LONELINESS: A FORCE TO RECKON

WILLIAM RICHARD BROWN

RoseDog Books

PITTSBURGH, PENNSYLVANIA 15238

RoseDog Books
585 Alpha Drive
Suite 103
Pittsburgh, PA 15238
Visit our website at *www.rosedogbookstore.com*

ISBN: 979-8-88604-611-3
eISBN: 979-8-88604-695-3

LONELINESS: A FORCE TO RECKON

TABLE OF CONTENTS

PREFACE:

Someone said, Find a subject that everyone has in common and write a book about it. I chose loneliness as that topic when I decided to write *Loneliness: A Force To Reckon*. I brought the word to life and I gave it character and a face, and named it Finn Bentley. He felt it deeply every day of his life, a conscious dogging that pursued him through the years.

Neither fame nor worldly success could ever satisfy in him the need to be loved and to belong. It is my hope that this book might make you more aware of the plight of the "Richard Corys" and the "Eleanor Rigby's" and Finn Bentleys" of the world, and be motivated to lend a hand to help lesson their burden as they are passing through. See Galatians 6:2.

CHAPTER 1.

THE CITY OF BROTHERLY LOVE

Except for one grim anomaly, Tuesdays have typically been my good news days. My fondest memories of life, joy, and peace can be traced back to that special day of the week. It was on a monarch wintry Tuesday morning when I first met the one who was to become my dearest friend and most intimate lover. While we were mere children, and struggling in the throes of elementary discovery, the unseen hand of fate brought us together and bonded us in an indissoluble union. He was eight and I was seven when like the opposite poles of a magnet, we were forged together in an inseparable attraction. Neither time nor circumstance could uncouple the force that had so wonderfully made us one in those early days of our childhood. We believed that nothing on earth could disassemble what angels had put together with their careful loving hands. Even when our friendship spiraled downward for a season, the rule that love conquers all caused lingering love-lines to finally arc upward again, and for one year, we lived that blissful moment in time together.

But the old adage that all good things must eventually come to an end was never more sullenly manifested than on that third doleful Tuesday morning—the day of the Morgan's funeral, the saddest day of my life.

… … … …

But now two years have passed, and waiting in the wings of the Providential Plan of Life, a new stage is being set. It opened on a brand new Tuesday morning as I stood precariously caught off balance, with one foot in the shower stall, and the other on the slick marble bathroom floor of our apartment. I was patiently waiting for the cold water from the spigot to turn warm when the phone in the living room rang. Isn't that always the way. All morning, the phone was mute. Now at the least opportune moment it chooses to send out it's annoying ring, demanding my attention.

Okay, why fight it? I turned off the water and went to answer.

"Hello," I said, trying to put forth my cheeriest voice and hoping this wasn't another pesky call from a telemarketer.

"Hello! May I speak with Phineas Bentley?"

"This is he," I answered cautiously.

"Hello, Mr. Bentley, this is Samuel Elkins, with the Bernard-Severson Corporation. Please pardon me if I'm calling too early in the morning, but I wanted to catch you before you went out. I was just now looking over your application for employment, and I must say that I was very much impressed by the extraordinary résumé you submitted. Would you be able to come in for an interview sometime this week?"

"Yes! I'd be delighted," I responded, trying not to sound too eager. "I have some free time tomorrow morning. Would that work for you?"

"That will be fine, Say about 10:30. Just come in the front door of the Butler Building. Take the elevator to the seventeenth floor and my secretary will be waiting to show you into my office. I'll be looking forward to meeting with you. See you then, goodbye."

He ended the conversation kind of abruptly, and I got the impression right off that Mr. Elkins was a man of succinct speech, especially when conducting matters of business. I would have to remember that in tomorrow's interview.

I wrote the appointment info on the desk calendar next to the phone, and then jumped back in the shower to finish what I had started out to do. Mom would be coming home from shopping soon and I was excited to give her the good news about being considered for a job with Bernard-Severson Corporation.

Mom was still a very attractive woman at the young age of fifty, the new forty, and was always an early riser, a habit she acquired from working the family business in Newton all those years. Now, in Philly, she had developed an M.O. of going out grocery shopping early and returning when I was still in bed and just pulling the sheets down off of my sleepy face. However, today I was erect, dressed, and finished with my morning ablutions early for a change.

We moved here to Philadelphia a year ago after she sold the

business to another family member for 3.5 million dollars. Along with the equity from the sale of our house at Briarwood Estates, we were sitting pretty sound financially, and would not have to worry about money ever again. Mom always has a good business sense and knew how to use the tax laws to her advantage. She keenly invested a large amount in diversified holdings with Benjamin Colliers and Associates. Her stocks and bonds alone generated enough dividends and interest from which we could draw a handsome income without ever even having to touch the principal. That, plus the salary I was drawing from my freelance journalism position with a well-known national magazine, we were able to afford a fancy apartment in Bonnieville Arms on Ridge Avenue, a wealthy section of Philadelphia. Working for the magazine kept me semi-occupied, but still left me with too much free time, and my old nemesis loneliness, with its insidious hounding, was always waiting to dog my every idle moment. By working at Bernard-Severson, I would be able to implement their structured workday as a healthful distraction in fighting against my frequent fits of depression. For there were times when missing Jake became so severe that like the surviving partner in Poe's poem, "Annabel Lee, " I would drive back to Newton and visit his grave in Augustine Memorial Cemetery. I'd sit there and talk to him for hours about how much I missed him and whatever was relevant to my recent emotional state. The thought of ever being intimate with someone else again seemed like a betrayal to him that my mind was unwilling to accept, and so loneliness perpetuated its unremitting grip on my heart. I was straddled with the impossible hope, could love ever conquer me twice? Could the fond caress of another male once again vanquish loneliness and sorrow?

Then came that night...and that dream...

... ...

"Phineas, I'm home," Mom greeted me as she came through the front door.

Her greeting jarred me awake from pensive memories of past events and returned my focus to the more imminent present.

"Mom! I've got some good news to share with you."

"Really! Well don't keep me in suspense," she said, excitedly. "What is it?"

"I just got a call from one of the job applications I sent out. Sam Elkins from Bernard-Severson just called me in for an interview. They're an advertising firm."

"That's wonderful, Phineas. Are you going to tell them you're gay?"

Mom had a way of being blunt which could be disconcerting at times, but in this context I considered it a fair question.

"Not unless it comes up. I prefer to keep it private, but I am not going to hide it either if they inquire."

"I'd be interested to know how they approach it," Mom added contemplatively.

"Mom! If anything like that gets discussed, I promise to give you a vivid description. Now, what do you say I put my culinary skills to work on breakfast?"

Suddenly, Mom surprised me with the suggestion that we order breakfast delivered from Cavacinni's Italian-American Cuisine.

"This calls for a celebration," she announced, and quickly made her way to the phone and ordered two full breakfasts before I could stop her. "Yes, ham and cheese omelets, and two sides of bacon and sausage. Oh, and two cannolis" (her personal favorites). She gave them the address and hung up the phone and announced, "If we're going to celebrate, we're going to do it right."

"I haven't even got the job yet, Mom."

"Oh, that's a slam dunk," she said convinced.

Her use of such a modern colloquialism made me chuckle to my myself.

"Once they meet with you and discover your knowledge and aptitude, gay or no gay, they'll snatch you right up and consider themselves fortunate to have you."

Spoken like a true mother. Although I felt confident that I could do whatever task they set before me to do, and do it well, I still battled periodically with the old unreasonable fear of being a social misfit. Without Jake's constant support I still struggled with the dreaded notion that others could not love me.

CHAPTER 2.

THE INTERVIEW

Wednesday morning, 10:25, I stood outside the front entrance of the Butler Building facing two tall glass revolving doors. It was one of the smaller skyscrapers with its 32 stories. The proud boast of the city of brotherly love is the Comcast building eclipsing the Philadelphia skyline with its 59 stories. But the Butler Building has an unequaled architectural uniqueness that distinguishes it from the other giants that encircle it. I had only to pass blithely through one of its two tall glass revolving doors when I was pleasantly struck by the amazing beauty of its impressively sculptured brass lobby. To my left were two crystalline glass-sided elevators which were designed to present a breathtaking view of the city as they rose upward along the periphery of the building's exterior glass walls which scaled from street level to the building's steel pinnacle. A slight pivot to the left placed me directly in front of the lift door. The entrance opened and the operator glanced at me and smiled. He looked to be an elderly gentleman in his sixties.

"Good morning! Where are you going, sir?" he asked in a polite voice.

"Bernard-Severson, seventeenth floor please, Ben," I responded, noticing his name tag

He smiled and asked, "And your name, sir?"

"Phineas Bentley," I answered, trying to put forth a confident demeanor.

"Happy to meet you, Mr. Bentley."

Whenever anyone addressed me with the title Mister, it felt like a moniker foreign to my identity, one that I wasn't qualified to wear, but not to confuse him, I accepted his greeting politely. When we got to the seventeenth floor and the door opened, I was pleasantly surprised that Bernard-Severson took up the whole floor. It had floor-to-ceiling glass windows around the whole perimeter, which permitted an excellent view of Philadelphia proper from all directions. In less than half a minute, a tall woman professionally dressed in a business suit approached me and introduced herself.

"Mister Bentley. I'm Ms. Vandevere, Mister Elkin's secretary. He's been expecting you. If you'll just follow me I'll show you into his office."

She led me to Sam Elkin's office without speaking—not even so much as a how do you do, which I thought would have been normal protocol. We went through some exquisitely carved oak doors into a spacious office with a high ceiling. At the far end there was a long mahogany desk behind which sat a nice looking gentleman who looked to be in his late fifties. He arose from behind his desk when he saw me enter the room.

Ms. Vandevere escorted me to him and did the introductions.

"Mr. Elkins, this is Mr. Bentley," she said politely, then turned and left without saying another word.

Mr. Elkins rose from his chair and extended his right arm to shake my hand.

"Good morning, Mr. Bentley, it's a pleasure to meet you." Then he picked up a file folder, came around his desk, led me to a sofa, and invited me to sit down. He chose to sit in an overstuffed chair directly across from me.

"You musn't mind Camilla, she can be a bit too stuffy at times. May I call you Phineas?"

"Call me Finn. I like that better and it's less formal," I said, hoping to lead out with a friendly icebreaker.

"Excellent, you can call me Sam. Although you'll notice that all the other employees refer to me as Mr. Elkins, I feel I already know you well enough by your résumé to extend to you that special courtesy."

"Thank you, Sam," I said respectfully. "I'm honored."

"I must say I was quite impressed with the application you submitted," he continued. "Your scholastic record is superb. It's no wonder that you were chosen the valedictorian of your class. And let me see now, you are currently doing freelance editorial work with *Brainstorm Quarterly Magazine*. Is that right?"

"Yes, that's correct. I've been writing for them for one year now."

"I have just a few questions to ask you that I was curious about if you would permit to be a bit more personal," he said cautiously.

"Please feel free to ask me anything you wish, Sam. It's probably best if we get it all out in the open now."

"Thank you, Finn. I admire your willingness to be candid. That's a quality hard to come by in today's younger generation."

He was looking in my file and thinking how to ask his question. "First of all, Finn, when I saw that you were valedictorian, I took the occasion to order a transcript of your speech for our records. I've read it and know all about your fight with gender confusion, and I want to say right off that it will not have any bearing on whether or not you are hired here. However, we do have a rule about employees dating each other within the company which is strictly observed."

"I fully understand, Sam, and that will not be a problem," I assured him.

"Good!" he continued gratefully. "Please forgive me, Finn, if I am prying too much into your private life, but I have one more question, and please feel free to decline from answering it if you'd rather not."

"Not at all, Sam, feel free to ask me anything," I offered.

"It says in your résumé that you've been working at the magazine for one year now, but what happened during the interim between your graduation and the time the magazine picked you up? You left that period curiously blank and I found that to be intriguing. Would you mind sharing?"

He probably wondered why I fell silent for a full minute while I formulated my answer. When I was reasonably satisfied with my reply, I began with my relationship with Jake.

"Back in the summer of 2017, I was reconciled in an association with my childhood sweetheart after a six-year breach in our relationship and for one whole glorious year we enjoyed a most beautiful love affair. Tragically, like so many beautiful things in life, it came to an abrupt end when my lover and his father were killed two days before graduation in a head-on collision by a drunk driver. I did my best to bear up under the weight of grief that threatened to overwhelm me until graduation, and the funeral was over, but then the initial shock wore off and the reality of it all threw me into a heavy depression and made me an emotional cripple for one whole year. Then during one of the few nights I was able to sleep, I had a dream about Jake. He came to me and took me in his loving arms. My body was as cold as ice, and I could actually feel the warmth of his embrace. He said he didn't want me to be sad and lonely but that he wanted me to be happy, even if it meant finding comfort in the arms of another lover. Then he kissed me and all my sadness and loneliness dissipated. It was so real I could actually feel his lips pressing on mine, and his tender words of comfort calming my spirit. Suddenly it was over and I awoke and found that it was morning. From that day forward the heaviness was lifted, and for the first time in a year, I felt a new resolve to move forward again. That's when I applied with *Brainstorm Quarterly* and was commissioned by them to write an article for each new issue about new emergent products and how they are advancing technology in today's world."

Sam sat there politely listening to my story, his sober expression not betraying his thoughts. When he finally spoke, I was grateful to discover him to be a man capable of deep sympathy and compassion.

"My son, how ever did you keep it all together during those few days of the graduation and the funeral?" he asked incredulously. "You have got to be a person of strong character to bear up under such a heavy weight of grief as that. No doubt your experiences have deepened you monumentally though I sense you've become a more sympathetic person now because of them. There are clients out there in the field who sometimes need a kindhearted human being like you to lean on for strength. And the kind of personal engagement you offer is what builds enduring business relationships. Yes, Finn! I believe that you're just the kind of person we would like working here. Would you consider coming to work for us at Bernard-Severson?"

"Allow me to say that since we talked on the phone yesterday, I've taken the opportunity to research Bernard-Severson on the net and have come to the decision that I'd be proud to work for your company," I said unequivocally. "But before I give you my final answer, may I inquire what my duties will be?"

"Yes! Well I'm sure you already know we're a marketing firm. Companies come to us for ideas on how to promote their products, which is something you are already doing with *Brainstorm Magazine*. We already have a team of people who write the ads. What will be expected of you, at least in the beginning, is to go out in the field and solicit new accounts. We usually send our people out in groups of two to meet with new clients. In your case you will be paired with my son Devin. He has a desk out in the front room, but you will occupy your own office next to mine. There is a front room entrance and there is also a side door directly to my office for additional duties for which you may be called on to perform. I will let you know what they are when and if the need arises. Does this meet with your approval so far?

"Yes, Sam. That is perfectly acceptable with me. When do I start?" I tried not to allow my curiosity to his secret condition be too noticeable, but my efforts were to no avail.

"Let's see, today is Wednesday. Why don't we make your starting date next Monday at ten o'clock. That way you can begin afresh at the beginning of the week. Devin will be here that day also and you two can meet. And one more thing, if you were wondering if my intentions about those additional duties could be less than honorable, I can assure you that I am straight, and always have been all my life, so you will not be called upon to do anything that would compromise your good character. I was a happily married man for 25 years before my wife passed, and have one son in which I am well pleased. I would never do anything to make him ashamed of me."

I blushed, and he gave out a snicker to let me know he knew what I was thinking. I learned then that I was not the only intuitive one in the room; Sam was also a student of perceptivity. Whatever Sam referred to as "those additional duties," it must be something virtuous, but best kept private for the present. There was a deep trust and admiration already forming in my opinion about this new human being coming into my life named Sam. In the short time I had gotten to know him, I already dared to relate to him as the warm father figure I never knew growing up. He had a way of making me feel totally accepted and trusted, which instilled in me the ardent desire to always please him with my best job performance.

"Monday morning it is then," he said. "I'll be looking forward to your working with us Finn, and may I add it has been a pleasure meeting you today."

We stood and shook hands and said our goodbyes. On my way to the elevator, Ms. Vandevere intercepted me in the open aisle to fill me in on a very helpful fact.

"Mr. Bentley, I thought that you should know that the third

floor of the adjacent parking garage is reserved for executive parking only. You can access it through the employees elevator on the wall at the east end of the office."

"Thank you, Ms. Vandevere. That was very kind of you. I'll be sure to use it when I come to work Monday."

"I've taken the initiative to assign #17 as your space number, she continued. As an extra courtesy, I've arranged for Alex our maintenance person to show it to you on your way down today."

Then, before I could say that won't be necessary, she turned and walked back to her desk without so much as a customary goodbye.

Alex looked to be about 30 years old and seemed friendly enough when he met me at the elevator. He was dressed in a dark blue maintenance uniform, probably provided him by the company. When he shook my hand I noticed he had an ugly red burn mark on his forearm just above his right hand.

"Ooh, Alex, that's a pretty serious burn you've got there. Have you sought any medical attention about it," I asked sympathetically. "You really should have it looked after so that it doesn't get infected."

"No! It's nothing major," he explained calmly. "It's just a little accident I suffered yesterday when I was cooking some steaks at home on the patio grill."

His injury looked to be round and deep, not the sort of mark that a live coal would make. Also, I couldn't imagine how it burned the top of his arm and not the underside, which seemed more plausible. At any rate, I decided not to question him further about it. I didn't want to appear nosey and make an enemy before my first day on the job.

The elevator door opened, and we walked through it together. The aperture was wide enough to accommodate three or more people entering at the same time. Curiously, Alex rubbed his side against mine in a deliberate manner as he made his way to press the floor selection button on the keypad. Suspicious thoughts immediately stirred up my intuition as I looked up into his face shooting him a puzzling glance, but he offered no explanation. Could it be that during this one brief encounter he had guessed what I am? The corners of his lips curled into a sly smile as he turned his head away, looking straight ahead, and waiting for the cage door to close and make the descent to the third floor.

"As you can see, Mr. Bentley, there are space numbers written on the side walls around the room. This is #17 and it is assigned to you. Mr. Elkins must think highly of you to assign you all these amenities so close to your initial hiring date," he said with a suspicious note in his voice. My mind immediately began processing this new information as I wondered how much he knew about me, how he knew it, and why he was so interested. The only two people who knew about my being gay were Sam and me, or so I thought. But in order to avoid further confrontation I chose not to comment or volunteer any more information to him.

"How do I get to the main elevators from here?" I asked, changing the subject.

He pointed to a door with a lighted red exit sign above it. "You can use that door to access the stairwell that runs up and down the whole east side of the building, or you can follow the hallway around to the public elevators which will take you down to the street level where you first entered."

"Thanks, Alex! I can find my way from here. I won't be needing any further assistance." At that I quickly turned and walked toward the exit door. Once through, I followed the hall around, as instructed, to the main elevators, and pressed the button with the little down arrow. A few seconds later I heard a ping sound and the door slid open. To my delight I was looking into the congenial face of Ben smiling down at me.

"Ah! Mr. Bentley, we meet again. Where can I take you to this time?

"You can take me down to the first floor level, Ben."

Thankfully, to my great relief, I felt calm and safe again as I boarded the car with friendly Ben at the controls. He smiled his friendly smile and hit button number one.

On the way down, my whole perspective started recovering peaceful thoughts. My mind started skipping ahead. I've sure got a lot to share with Mom when I get back home this afternoon.

CHAPTER 3.

CLOTHES MAKE THE MAN?

"Mom! I'm home!" It was always our policy to shout out our arrival when coming in the apartment front door. Residing in Philadelphia was not like our previous residence in the safe little town of Newton where everyone knew one another on the block. Even though Bonnieville Arms had beefed up its security, with a man at the front desk 24/7 and a security guard, still there was always the possibility of an intruder bypassing all the prophylactics and showing up at the front door of your apartment unannounced. Mom came rushing out of her office at the sound of my announcement.

"Phineas, thank heavens you're back. I've been waiting all morning to hear how your interview went with Bernard-Severson. Sit down here on the sofa and tell me all about it. Did you get the job? What will you be doing? What about your boss? Is he married? Is he handsome? Did you tell him you're gay?"

"Whoa, Mom!" I said, amused at her enthusiasm. "One thing at a time. Be patient and I'll answer all your questions to your complete satisfaction. First of all, I did get the position, and it is better than I could ever have imagined. I start on Monday and I will have my own office next to my boss, Sam Elkins—who, by the way, is a handsome widower in his early fifties. I was hired as an ad exec and will be actively visiting and bringing in new clients. Sam said I would be working with his son Devin, whom I have not yet met. And yes the subject of my alternate lifestyle was approached and discussed. It seems Sam ordered a transcript of the valedictorian speech I gave at Newton High. Hence, very few explanations were needed before I got there. I'll tell you more about that some other time."

I decided to keep from Mom the little detail about the mysterious door arrangement between our offices. I didn't want her to worry about it unnecessarily. Also the encounter with Alex the maintenance man I decided to keep quiet also.

"Well, is there anything I can do to help you get ready during the hiatus between now and Monday?" she asked, using her higher

English vocabulary.

"Yes, Mom, there is. I'm going to need you to come shopping with me for some formal clothes, suits, shirts, ties, and shoes. Also some casual, but tasteful, attire. In short I'm going to need a complete wardrobe change. I've never been one to pay attention to current styles so I will have to rely heavily on your expertise on how to dress to make the best impression in the business world."

Mom was chomping at the bit and rearing to go, but I had to slow her down.

"I'd be better prepared to start shopping tomorrow, besides, we can get an early start and make a full day of it."

I noticed the disappointment on Mom's face. Ever since she sold the business, and we moved here, she was suffering from cabin fever, and now with me going to be away at work every day, I was afraid she would start to stagnate. I realized I would have to take up the gauntlet and find ways for her to get involved socially before she sank too deeply into a slump.

"How about going to Cracker Barrel for lunch today?" I suggested. "And then take in a movie at the Paramount? I've heard there's a good chick flick playing there."

She flashed her suspicious smile at me but agreed reluctantly. If I could have read her mind, she would be thinking, "Oh, Phineas, you're so predictable!" Then as I had predetermined, the remainder of the day was devoted to keeping her occupied. That night, before I closed my eyes to sleep, I wished I could see Jake again in my dreams. I had so much to talk with him about. But the only compensation that sleep brought that night was a full night's rest and the replenished energy needed to go clothes shopping with mom.

We left the apartment building at 9:30 a.m., Thursday morning and headed north in the RAV4. There was a convenient parking garage close to the Second and Third Streets in Philadelphia's Old City. We could use the car as a locker to return to repeatedly and stash our mounting purchases. Mom was an amazing shopper when she went into action. She had the day all planned out, and what ordinarily would have taken me eight hours to accomplish, she had condensed into four hours of easy visitations to the best specialty shops in the city. Before heading home, we decided to dine at one of Philadelphia's finer restaurants for a nice sit down dinner.

"This looks like a nice place to eat," Mom said consulting the data on her smart phone. "Alberto's, let's try it."

Shopping for clothes was among my least favorite things to do, so being able to sit down and rest sounded wonderful to me. If she had picked McDonalds, I would have been just as agreeable, but Italian cuisine was among my second most preferred choices. Mexican food was at the top of the list. For a minute, my mind went back to how much Jake and I liked Taco Bell. Time is supposed to bring healing, but I wondered. Will I ever stop missing him?

Since it was early Thursday afternoon and the evening crowd hadn't come in yet, the place was pretty much empty, and we were able to be seated quickly. Our waiter, a handsome, young, well-built Italian boy came over to our table and handed us our menus. He looked about 20 years old and had a slight trace of a European accent.

"Good evening, my name is Georgio, and I'll be your waiter tonight. Is there anything I can get you to drink while you're looking over the menu?"

Mom and I said, "Just water," at the exact same time and chuckled. The waiter left and returned with a pitcher of water, bread sticks, and small bowl with olive oil mixed with spices for dipping. We gave him our order and handed back the menus. When he took mine, he deliberately rubbed his hand against mine and smiled to send me a sexy signal. Try as I might to not let it affect me, nevertheless it did. Temptations to dwell on fantasies indulging liaisons with other men was best kept at bay, and not allowed to draw me into a damaging promiscuous lifestyle. There were no more incidences until it was time to go. He was standing at the door and thanked us for coming to Alberto's, and when he shook my hand he slipped a little piece of paper to me. While Mom hailed a cab to take us back to the parking garage, I unfolded and read it. He had printed his contact information on it, phone number, his name Georgio, and the words "Call me." I put it in my pocket with the intent of throwing it in the trash later.

When we finally got back in the RAV4 and were headed home, Mom called ahead on her cell phone for Jimmy to meet us in the private parking garage at our reserved space. Jimmy was a cute 14-

year-old boy who lived on the first floor with his uncle and made extra money by carrying in packages for tenants. We had several shopping bags full and five full suits on hangers. Mom was a good tipper, so Jimmy was happy to be of service whenever she called. On the rare occasions when I called on him for help and I tried to tip him he would not take the money. He said he was happy to give me his aid for free. It wasn't hard to guess that he had a crush on me, but he was still too young and inexperienced to be an active pursuant. Nevertheless, because of my past history of emotional bruisings, I felt enough empathy to handle him gently and with kid gloves, to use the trite pugilistic term. Teenagers his age can be very fragile, and I wouldn't want to cause injury to his young sensitive male ego. Jimmy's uncle, whom he lived with, was a wealthy retiree. He insisted Jimmy develop his entrepreneur skills while still young so that when he got older, he would be able to make his own way in the world without having to depend on others.

As soon as we arrived and parked, we got out of the car, gave Jimmy the keys to lock up, and headed for the elevator. Mom and I had just stepped into the lift when I spied a suspicious man wearing a black hoodie at the opposite end of the parking garage. He was looking right at us, but when he saw that I had noticed him, he moved behind a concrete pillar before I could get a good look at his face.

Later, back in the apartment, when all the purchases were delivered, Mom unpacked them and put them into my walk-in closet, being careful to arrange them perfectly color coordinated. She took all the guesswork out of my dressing by putting suits, shirts, and ties together and assigned them for each day of the week. All the casuals were put on one rack in the other side of the closet and arranged in the same meticulous order. The unreasonable fear of a misfit entering the workforce was slowly seducing my brain and causing my anxiety level to peak. To keep my mind off of developing stress factors associated with the job, I decided to stay busy looking for ways to get Mom involved with the other ladies in the building.

Through Roger the doorman I discovered that one of them on the sixth floor led a book club discussion group every Wednesday afternoon, and also hosted group bus trips now and then. They had planned an upcoming overnighter to NYC to see a Broadway musical. Now all I had to do was to get Mom to join them and make her think it was her own idea. Roger gave me a pamphlet they had made up to give out to any of the tenants who might be interested in joining. The rest was easy. I went back up the apartment and left the flier on the living room end table where Mom was sure to see it. It was as simple as catching fish with dog food for bait.

"Phineas! What is this about a book club here in the complex? Where did you get this pamphlet?"

"Roger the doorman gave it to me 'cause he knows how much I love reading, but now that I am going to be at work when they meet I won't be able to attend. I meant to throw it away but just hadn't gotten around to it yet."

"Well I'm glad you didn't," said Mom chastising. "This could be something to help occupy my time while you're at work."

"Yes, that's true. I didn't even think of it that way," I said, secretly musing. "Why don't you give them a call and introduce yourself and tell them you'd be interested in joining them."

Avis Fullerton, the leader of the book club, was overjoyed to have Mom come and join their little group, and also told Mom about some other activities in which she might also like to get involved. In no time at all, she and Avis were on their way to becoming best friends.

Mission accomplished. Now I could relax and just concentrate on getting mentally ready to report to work next week. Just five days off and how I wished it was Monday already.

CHAPTER 4

MONDAY: WHO IS DEVIN?

At exactly ten o'clock I anxiously stepped out of the open elevator door into the company of Bernard-Severson for the first time as an employee. Ms. Vandervere was waiting to extend her usual formal friendless greeting minus the "how do you do?"

"Good morning, Mr. Bentley, Mr. Elkins would like to see you before you head to your office. Please follow me, sir." Again she led me into Sam's office, and after announcing my arrival, promptly left.

"Hello, Finn! I wanted to visit with you a few short minutes before you go to your office. You won't be going out to visit any clients today. I feel that you could use one day to familiarize yourself with a copy of our client list and spend the day getting to know Devin. He will be here at 10:30."

"Sure, Sam. Whatever you think is best."

"Good! The list is on your office desk; you can enter through the adjoining door between our offices. There is one thing I need to make clear to you. Every day between 3:00 to 4:00, Ms. Vandervere will come into my office, and during that time, my doors will be locked. No one else will be admitted during that time. Are we clear on that?"

"Perfectly, Sam," I said, wondering what all the secrecy was about, but reminding myself that it was none of my business, and it was best for me just to blindly follow his instructions for the present.

"You may go now. Devin will be with you shortly."

While I was waiting for Devin in my office, my mind went back to what my thoughts were on the first day I met Jake, when we were kids. Is he cute, will he like me? Was I starting to forget him? Was this what he wanted for me when he told me he didn't like seeing me sad and lonely? While all these nondescript thoughts were bouncing around in my brain, there was a knock on the door that led to the outer office.

"Come in," I said.

In walked a strikingly handsome Devin with a shocked look on his face as soon as he saw me at my desk. His eyes went wide open and his face took on a blank stare as when the mind slips into the instant recognition of a past event being portrayed in lucid repetition. He looked strangely familiar, but for the life of me I could not place him. But that was not the case with him; he seemed to recognize me right off.

"Hi!" I said. "I'm Finn Bentley; you must be Devin. Have we met before? I said, curiously. "You look familiar."

"Uh, I'm sure if I met someone as cute as you before, I wouldn't soon forget it," he said evasively.

Okay! His dad must have given him the heads up about my being gay or why else would he refer to me as being cute, but I decided to let it slide for the present.

"It's almost lunchtime," he continued. "How about getting to know one another better over lunch."

"Sure," I answered, pretending not to be affected by his forward approach. "Where do you have in mind to eat? Are there any good fast food places close by?" I suggested.

"Oh no, you're an executive now," he said. "We'll eat at Mitzy's and have a nice sit down lunch at a private booth where we can get better acquainted," he said in a seemingly seductive manner. "It'll be my treat for your first day here."

... ...

From the minute we walked into Mitzy's, the male receptionist and the female waitress recognized him and made it a point to give him their personal attention along with showering him with their shameful flirtatious advances. Sure he was handsome, and that I was willing to admit, but already my first impression of him was that he didn't need any more encouragement to increase his hat size.

He whispered something to the receptionist and we were ushered to a private booth with no other patrons close by. I kept trying to recall where our paths could have crossed.

"Dad thought we should get to know each other so he gave me

your complete résumé to read over the weekend. I hope you don't think I would use your information to promote feelings of prejudice against you."

"Well, I don't mind you knowing my history, since I've nothing to hide, but I feel now you have a slight advantage on me since I don't know anything about you."

"There's not much to know. I'm the boss's son, I've had two years of education at a junior college in which Dad paid for my tuition, but I insisted he didn't pay for any of my other expenses. I got a job and supported myself. All my housing, food, and clothing expense I paid for out of the money I made working."

At first it sounded to me like he was being boastful about his independence, but then I chastised myself for my critical thinking.

"Where did you go to college?" I asked, trying to change the subject.

"Routers Business School, in Dobersville," he said with a reticent smile.

When he mentioned Dobersville, I immediately connected that with the same area as the Morgan's cabin. My suspicions started to raise, and I decided to query him further.

"Where did you work in Dobersville?" I asked suspiciously, trying not to appear too inquisitive.

"Several different jobs, but mostly at fast food places as a delivery boy."

Suddenly the connection was made as it all came back vividly into my recollection—the night I stepped outside to pay the handsome Taco Bell driver and his sneaky kiss. A smile of knowing he had been found out came across Devin's face. My next question I asked cautiously, not wanting it to sound too accusatory and spoil our new business partnership.

"When I asked you if we had met before, why did you lie to me, and say we never met?"

"No, I didn't lie. What I said was, 'If I met someone as cute as you, I would not soon forget it,' and I haven't. But you can imagine my surprise meeting up with you in your office today, and realizing my good fortune to be working with you at Bernard-Severson. It's pure kismet. I cannot explain it any other way," he said convincingly.

When he explained it that way, I couldn't help but chuckle, try as I might to be sober faced. Between my relief that he hadn't lied to me and his confession of not being able to forget that kiss, I had to agree that there certainly was something at work between us. If not random fate, then it had to be divine providence; blaming it on mere coincidence would be too naive.

"However, please forgive me if I'm intruding into your private life," he continued, "but what happened between you and Jake?"

"How did you know his name was Jake?" I asked.

"Everybody at Taco Bell knew his first name from coming in to get food so often and having to call it out when his order was ready."

Obviously Sam had not given Devin that little bit of personal information, which added to my growing respect for his being able to keep a confidence. My eyes started to tear and my throat choked up as I told Devin about the accident that claimed the lives of Jake and his father two days before our high school graduation.

"I'm sorry to hear that about him; he was the nicest one who came into the place and also the most generous tipper whenever I delivered to the cabin. But let me say this, for you to stand up and give that inspiring valedictorian speech two days after losing the guy you loved more than anyone else in the world would take someone with extraordinary strength of character. My respect for you as a person has just grown much deeper now that I've listened to you share your story. I'm proud to have you as a working partner in the sales department of Bernard-Severson. I think we will be able to form a good alliance in the field, and I hope also that we can grow to be close friends on and off the job."

Nothing more was said about the kiss, and for the present I thought it better to suspend the whole incident until a later discussion.

When we got back to the seventeenth floor, we went to our separate desks and I used the rest of the time to study the next day's client list. Googling the profile of an ad agency proved to be helpful in developing the next day's strategy.

Devin left early in the afternoon without any explanation of where he was going. Then promptly at 3:00, Camilla put a sign on her desk that said closed, and went into Sam's office. Seconds later I heard a clicking sound of the door locking between me and them. If nothing else this job was surely not lacking in mystery. My workday concluded at 4:00 p.m., and I headed for the employees elevator that took me down to the parking garage where I now had my own reserved space. This floor in the garage was only for executives and at the moment was quite deserted. No sooner had I started walking toward my car when I spied someone in a dark hoodie walking toward me. He looked just like the one I saw at the apartment garage last Wednesday. Two things struck me as odd. One, he wasn't dressed like an executive and two, he was suspiciously heading right at me. Also there was something partially concealed in his right hand which I couldn't precisely identify at first until it had later filtered again through my recall. Suddenly the elevator door opened again and three more people entered the garage, which startled the intruder who quickly turned and fled down the stairwell. I immediately began analyzing what had just happened and my assessment of the event started taking on an alarming perspective. Two men in dark hoodies? Two different garages? Both connected to me and my lifestyle? And judging from this last sighting, he was intent on making some kind of contact with me. Maybe it was time to alert the police about a stalker. Believe me, I'm not one to neglect priorities, but it had been a tiring day, so I chose to let it go for the present until tomorrow.

CHAPTER 5

BRIEFING MOM

"Hi, Mom, I'm home!" I hollered out our usual greeting.

She came running out of her office with an inquisitive look written all over her face, and a list of questions on her mind that required prompt answers.

"Phineas, I've been waiting impatiently all day to hear how your first day went. Did you meet the boss's son? Is he handsome? What is he like? And did you say that Sam Elkins is a widower? Is he attractive? Do you think there's enough to do in this job to keep you interested?"

"Mom! Slow down. You're changing subjects faster than a Jehovah's Witness. I'm happy to answer all your questions, but let me choose the order." At that she settled down and I began to recount the day's occurrences.

"First, yes Sam Elkins is a very attractive man, and yes he is a widower."

Wheels obviously began turning in Mom's head, and I couldn't help but admit that sometimes both our minds ran in the same female thought lanes.

"His son Devin is very handsome too, and I have some startling news to relay about that in a little bit. We haven't gone out into the field together yet, but we are scheduled to do a visit tomorrow with an important client. There is a lot of secrecy going on that I'm not given the privilege yet of knowing. As the feds would put it, it's above my pay grade." With that I confided in Mom about the locked door between Sam's office and mine between 3:00 and 4:00 every day, and how Ms. Vandevere is the only one allowed in there.

"That is a mystery," Mom explained, "but I'm sure it will be cleared up when you've been there a little longer. Things like that have a way of coming to light as time goes on."

"Thanks, Mom, I've come to the same conclusion. And now, the most amazing thing about meeting Devin is that we met before under quite different circumstances."

Now, I reasoned, it would be okay to let Mom in the loop about the delivery boy's kiss during that last Christmas with Jake at the cabin. And how Jake had just laughed it off and said it was my fault for being so damned cute, and how he joked about having to keep a closer eye on me from then on. Then when Devin walked into my office he recognized me right off, but I didn't recognize him until later in the day during lunch.

Mom's eyes got wide with excitement. "You mean Devin is the Taco Bell delivery boy who kissed you that day two years ago? Could that be a sign that you two were meant for each other? How else can you explain your being put together again at the same time in a big city like Philadelphia so far from Dobersville and two years later."

"For sure," I agreed. "It could be a classic case of serendipity, but for now I'm content to wait and see how it all plays out. Devin described it as kismet. Now, there is one more mystery I feel I must let you in on in case it develops into something serious and you should find yourself in danger."

"Oh! What's that, dear?" Mom said with keen interest.

"It first happened last Wednesday night when we were coming home from shopping and Jimmy met us down in the parking lot to carry in the packages. You didn't notice it because you had your back turned when the elevator door was closing behind us, but I spied a mysterious man in a black hoodie looking out at us from behind a concrete pillar at the far end of the garage. When he saw that I saw him, he ducked behind the pillar before I could get a good look at his face."

"That doesn't sound so serious, Phineas. It could be explained by any number of things."

"That's what I originally thought too, until the same person appeared in the vacant garage at the Butler Building today and was walking right toward me until the elevator opened and some execs entered the floor. As soon as he saw them he turned and fled down the stairwell."

"Oh my, that is ominous," Mom warned. "You should report it to the police. It could be a stalker or something. You're not even sure if it was a man or a woman. They could have had a gun, a knife, or even a taser. At least if you notify the police they will have something to go on if it happens again. But thanks for giving me the heads-up. I'll be on the lookout for any strange people from now on. My! You really have had an interesting day."

This latest item of a possible stalker brought an added complication in my life that I didn't need right now. Focusing on giving my undivided attention to Bernard-Severson required a large amount of conscious energy to ensure that I'd be giving Sam my promised best performance. Now I found myself also having to contend with a mysterious adversary who may be intent on causing me physical harm. Contacting the police seemed like the best course of action and one on which would be wise not to further procrastinate.

The phone at the desk in the 17th precinct rang at about 7:00 p.m.

"Hello! Police station. Sergeant Connors speaking. May I help you."

"Yes, I hope you can. My name is Phineas Bentley, and I'd like to report a suspicious person following me."

"Well, Mr. Bentley, I'm just the desk clerk here. I suggest you come in and see Lt. Myerson and fill out a report so that we'd have something to go on if anything more comes of it. Would you like to make an appointment?"

"Yes I would, but I'm employed so I'd have to schedule it around my work day activities."

"No problem, Lt. Myerson is usually here all day. Would you be able to come in at 5:00 tomorrow afternoon."

" Yes, Sergeant, that should work out quite nicely. See you then. Have a nice day!"

By the time I hung up the phone, I felt confident that things were coming under control, and that I had acted responsibly in handling the situation.

Mom and I had a late dinner. We ordered in Chinese food from the Singapore Sling down the block from our apartment building. Within 30 minutes we were sitting down at the table enjoying Moo Goo Gai Pan. I cautioned Mom not to let anybody new into the apartment until this whole curious business is resolved.

CHAPTER 6

TUESDAY: SECOND DAY AT WORK

My work day begins at 10:00 and I am always as punctual as possible barring any unforeseen circumstance. I was getting situated at my desk right on time when Devin Elkins walked in the door.

"Good morning, Mr. Elkins," I said.

"Please call me Devin," he instructed. "After all, we already have known each other intimately if you know what I mean."

His male assertiveness made me blush and there was no way to hide it. When he saw the effect he had on me, he was emboldened to instruct me further.

"Today we are visiting Sarah Bronson of Sarah's Home-baked Cookies. When we get there I'll do most of talking and you are to come along as an observer. Are you ready to go because our meeting is at 11:00 and their office is way across town? We'll go in my car and afterward we should have adequate time to grab lunch before we have to get back here again."

"I'm ready now," I said.

Like Jake, Devin was a man with a plan who liked to take charge, but I wasn't as comfortable with his leadership yet as I used to be with Jake; nevertheless, I surrendered to it. Devin wore his male identity confidently; it was a fact that the defense of his gender was not necessary with him. He was always comfortable and at home in his maleness, which made for a strong compatibility with his handsome attractiveness. For sure, he had more Y-chromosomes than I had and I knew I was no competition to his male confidence. Devin drove a cherry red Mustang convertible that enhanced his manly image so much that I almost felt like my femininity was being taken advantage of.

... ...

Sarah Bronson was an attractive thirty-six-year-old woman

who had built a million dollar business from her grandmother's cookie recipe. But when Sarah saw handsome Devin enter her office door I could tell she was instantly smitten. Devin's good looks made an obvious positive impression with the ladies, and when she saw that handsome face and those sparkling white teeth of his, together with that well-conditioned body that he sported, her warm acceptance extended us an open door. However, Bernard-Severson was also a highly respected marketing firm and already led the field with an impressive parade of happy clients, so when Devin got around to presenting the ad campaign that the department had come up with, I was encouraged to see that Sarah's final decision was the result of her well-founded business like rationale and not just a another victim of his captivatingly good looks.

Devin left the legal portion of the sale in my hands since I had a proficient background in business law through extracurricular studies I had done while I was still in high school. Business law was actually my second favorite study in school next to English literature. Actually I had enough under my belt to pass the bar exam in Pennsylvania if I had applied.

We left her with a copy of the contract to sign after she had time to go over it with her lawyers.

... ...

I could tell Devin was anxious to get to lunch so I asked him if he was hungry. His answer surprised me.

"You seem in a hurry to get to eat lunch. Are you very hungry?" I asked.

"Not particularly," he answered. "It's not the food that I'm craving today; it's the company."

It was an obvious hit, but I pretended not to notice it. However, he knew I had received it and shot me a sly smile. As much as I tried to ignore the attraction to his self-assured masculinity, the growing need for male affection was becoming increasingly more difficult to deny. Nevertheless I didn't want our relationship to degenerate into a selfish venue of mere mutual exploitation. I needed love more than I needed sexual gratification. and I was willing to hold out for the substantial rather than settle for some superficial act of temporary pleasure. I needed to give Devin more time to reveal his true motives whether benign or just in gaining another sexual conquest.

We drove back across town and decided to eat lunch at Mitzy's again. The same private table awaited u,s and I was grateful this time for the seclusion because I decided it was time for us to establish some safe boundaries of our working relationship. I had a lot of questions and I figured that now would be the perfect time to bring them up, but before I could get one out, Devin surprised me with a question that caught me completely unprepared.

He looked straight into my eyes with a serious expression on his face and asked, "Remember that night I pulled you into my arms on your front porch and kissed you? You probably thought of me as being forward or rude, but the truth is that I fell in love with you from that first glance I caught of you way back in September. I know it sounds crazy, the whole thing about love at first sight, but I can't help but believe we were somehow meant to be."

I started to say that I didn't mean to provoke his aggressive behavior in any way, but before I could speak, he continued.

"From that day on I kept a sharp lookout for any orders going to that cabin and told them all at the TB that if any orders came in from there that I wanted to be the one to deliver it. Then when the order from that cabin was called in on my last night on the job, I began planning my move. I felt that no matter how hopeless the circumstances seemed, I just had to let you know how much I cared about you. I thought, who knows, the situation between you and Jake could someday change, and I wanted to be around to pick up the pieces. Imagine my good luck when you came out to receive the delivery and I found myself alone with you on the front porch. I was so nervous and aroused that I responded out of sheer desperation. When my lips made contact with yours, I felt an instant transfer of affection and I couldn't help but feel that you felt it too. When I ran to my car and drove away, my head felt like it was sticking out of the clouds, my emotions were running high. Although, at that time, I thought it was hopeless to even wish for another meeting, but in the past two years my heart never ceased hoping that our paths would someday again intertwine."

He reached across the table and his hand gently covered over mine. My head was telling me to resist him; it was too soon to be plunging into another serious relationship, but that damn weakness of mine for sincerity was leading the way again, and my heart had no other option but to follow. Tears began flowing down my cheeks caused by this new verbal ambush at the heart level. He sat there looking intently into my watering eyes and waiting for my reply. Finally I choked out my first line of negative defense.

"But I promised Jake that I would never love another."

Devin must have anticipated some opposition on my part and he was prepared to handle all my objections.

"I can't begin to imagine how deep and wonderful your love was with Jake, nor would I presume to compare myself to him, but from what little I know of him, I'm sure he never meant your promise of celibacy to exceed the separation of death, or for you to live the rest of your life out in loneliness. Your desire to be faithful is highly commendable, and I love you the more for it. But think, Finn! If you had died instead of him, would you have wanted him to hold to his promise of celibacy for the rest of his lonely existence, or would you want him to go on living, even if that meant finding happiness again in the arms of someone else? Please, Finn! Give me the chance to be the one to fill that lonely void that you keep buried deep inside of you."

The depth of his insight eclipsed my own, and his arguments penetrated every protective wall I had set up in my heart. He gave my hand a gentle squeeze and then moved over beside me on the bench and kissed me lightly on the lips, and waited to observe any reluctance from me. Finding none, he then gave me a long lasting kiss, and I felt again that love transference that I had first felt that winter's night long ago on the porch at the cabin. All my defenses had fallen. My life had taken an unexpected turn, and this new second love was giving me the confidence I needed to believe that a misfit like myself could again find a home in the heart of another.

On our way back to the office in Devin's car, we sat in silence. My mind, however, was preoccupied trying to reconfigure my work situation given this new complication of an intimate relationship. Devin seemed to sense my apprehensiveness and spoke up first.

"If you're concerned with the rule about employee relationships, you needn't be. It only applies to straight couples. That's where we gays have the edge over them. Besides, we don't have to be out to our fellow employees about our secret love life, and if they suspect anything, let them wonder. They don't have any proof, and accusations without proof is grounds for immediate dismissal. Dad is a stickler about gossip not being tolerated among office workers. But now that you've allowed me into your life, do you mind my asking what you've planned to do for the rest of your day?"

The appointment with Lt. Myerson later today flashed through my mind, and I wondered how I was going to tell Devin about this recent glitch of being the target of a stalker. I started by relating the first account of his sighting in the parking garage at the apartments, but Devin didn't seemed to be too concerned until I mentioned seeing him the second time on the employee garage floor.

"Seriously, Finn, that's too weird. We need to report that to the police right away."

"I've already alerted them, and I have an appointment with the police detective this afternoon at five o'clock. Would you mind coming with me?"

"Absolutely, and I'll do better than that. I'll meet you in the garage when you arrive every morning and walk you to your car every night until this stalker is caught. I've waited for you too long to let you be harmed or abducted by some crazed lunatic. I'm so glad you told me about this. If anything happened to you now, I could never forgive myself."

"But what if he's packing a weapon, like a knife or a gun? I wouldn't want an injury or worse to happen to you on my account. A second grief from losing another lover would be a loss from which I don't think I could ever recover."

"Don't worry, I'm skilled in martial arts. I say this not to brag, but I've been taking classes at the dojo for five years now and am a grand master."

"Oh! That's where you've been going everyday at 3:30 when you leave the office. One mystery solved!"

"One mystery?" he asked puzzled!

"There's one more I'll have to keep to myself for the time being until I can uncover more of what it means."

CHAPTER 7

SECOND LUNCH AT MITZY'S

When I got back to work, there was a note on my desk saying I should see Sam Elkins in his office, ASAP. I entered through the connecting door between our offices. Sam was seated at his desk with a worried look on his face. I walked over in front of him and stood there waiting for him to speak. He got up and walked across the room and sat in the overstuffed chair and instructed me to lock both of the office doors before coming over to be seated across from him on the sofa. Once I sat down attentively across from him he began his long explanation of the secret duties he had mentioned during my job interview.

"Do you remember, Finn, when I told you that you may be asked to perform certain duties in the future, and that I would make known to you what they were if and when the need arose."

"Yes! I remember, Sam, and I want you to know that whatever it is I trust you implicitly and have put myself totally at your disposal."

"Thank you, Finn. It means a lot for me to know I can count on you."

He continued with labored speech. I surmised it was because of the emotional request he was about to lay on me.

"I had hoped that you would have had more time to get acclimated to your work duties here before I burdened you with this new responsibility. However, Camilla just notified me that a family emergency has recently arisen and that she would have to leave our employ to care for her spinster sister in Des Moines. It seems her car was struck by a teenager who ran a stoplight while texting. She sustained injuries that will require her to undergo a lengthy period of rehabilitation, and Camilla would have to care for her at home, and be available to transport her back and forth to rehab everyday. She informed me she would be leaving here at the end of the week. I have weekends covered by my driver who doubles as my gentleman's gentleman at home. Your extra duty will begin on Monday next week, that is, if you agree to help me out."

I sat quietly listening to his prelude before getting around to announcing the essentials. Then he looked me in the eyes, and with a heavy sigh, explained why such a huge commitment was necessary to be placed on my shoulders.

"About two years ago, Finn, between the hours of 3:00 and 4:00, I was in this office working when, for the first time, I experienced an epileptic seizure in which I suffered a loss of conscious awareness. Luckily, Camilla was in this office working with me at the time. Camilla had nurses training before she came to work for us so she knew the signs and just what to do. She remained cool-headed and wheeled my chair over next to the sofa, dumped me onto it, and covered me with a blanket to keep me warm and calm. In twenty minutes it passed, and I had fully recovered my composure. This same attack repeated itself once again the next week—curiously at the same time of day, but this time I was able to sense it approaching and notify Camilla in time that I needed help. Nevertheless, after the second occurrence, we both agreed I should consult a specialist and get professional advice on how to best treat my condition. To make a long story short, after all the results from the tests were in, it was diagnosed that I had a mild form of epilepsy that often manifested itself in patients between the age of 50 and 60 years of age. There was however one difference in my case that was one for the books—go figure. It was discovered that I have a unique brain function that makes it super sensitive to the lunar magnetic pull and its effect on atmospheric pressure. Although the lunar pull is constant, the atmospheric pressure fluctuates due to changing weather patterns, which accounts for my episodes occurring on random days of the week but always during a specific time period of the day. Both conditions have to occur simultaneously, and when they do, I have an attack. There is one other thing that you should know. As of now, the only ones who know of my condition are me, Camilla, and now you. It is important that no one else be privy to this information. If this news got out to members of the board, they may think that it might impair my job performance."

"Sam, I quite understand your concerns, and you can rely on me to assume these extra duties when Camilla leaves. I do however have one more question that I feel should be addressed."

"Certainly, what is it?" Sam said, anticipating, Then before I could ask it, he volunteered, "You're probably wondering about Devin."

"Yes, shouldn't he know about this in case it is hereditary?"

"Finn, I believe I can trust you so I am going to let you in on another closely guarded family secret. Soon after my wife Diane and I were married, she became pregnant and we were very excited to be having a child. We soon learned that it wasn't to be. In her third trimester she miscarried, and because of complications in the fetal extraction, it became known to us that she could not have any more children. We were both devastated by the sad news until we learned that another woman, with whom we were friends, also had become pregnant out of wedlock and was not willing to jeopardize her career by having to raise a child. When she heard about our misfortune, she contacted us and asked if we would take her baby. My wife and I talked it over and agreed as long as we could contact a lawyer to draw up the papers for a permanent legal adoption. She agreed to those terms, and we went through with the adoption of a baby boy whom you now know as Devin. His real mother provided us the name of his biological father whom we contacted and ran a check on his medical history. Both the mother and father were given a clean bill of health. As an extra precaution, we had him sign off on any claim to the child, which he was very willing to do. His real parents married shortly after. They were happy and content with the way their lives were going. And then tragedy struck. On September 11, 2001, they boarded United flight 93 in Newark on a business trip to San Francisco. It's all history now; it was one of three planes hijacked by al-Qaeda that later crashed in Stoneycreek, PA. We never told Devin he was adopted. With both biological parents now gone, there would be no point further to do so."

Here I sat, a young employee blindsided by all this new data which I wished I could have been more prepared. But instead, I found myself looking precariously into the face of a mature, successful businessman, and presuming I had something of significant worth to offer him as solid advice. Still, the necessity of divulging the information I held was gnawing on my conscience as I vacillated between two choices. One was to keep quiet and go with the flow. The other was to throw caution to the wind and undauntedly spout it out—even if it incurred the scorn of someone I was very fond of and who held my deepest respect.

"Sam! I realize the advice I am going to give you is unsolicited, but please believe me when I say I offer it to you with my humblest respect to your judgment. These secrets you have entrusted me with today are not two different issues, but one. First of all, I have in the past done studies in medical journals about epilepsy from the mildest to the more severe cases, and one thing they all agree upon is that it is progressive; however, the rapidity of increase is variable from one individual to another. We can hope that you have one of the slower, more static cases, but that may not be pre-diagnosed for certain. The reason I lay this groundwork before you is that in the unforeseen future it may become necessary to let Devin in on it so that he could gain the margin of expertise needed to efficiently profile your care, either directly or through the agency of professional care givers. Also, in the event this scenario ever arises, Devin would most certainly become curious about whether or not, health-wise, he would be at risk of inheriting it from you. At which time, the issue of his adoption would need to be disclosed to allay any fears he might have that in the future his own health could become compromised."

"Well, Finn, you have brought out quite skillfully a plan of action that heretofore I have been unwilling to think about," Sam said, admiringly. "I confess I've been selfish in not considering the future involvement of others someday having to be put in charge of my care."

"You need not worry about becoming burdensome, Sam. All the while you're not in an episode you are able to perform all duties entirely functional. The only necessary help you would be needing is during one of those random attacks, which for now Camilla can assist you with, and when she leaves, I will be happy to fill in the gap."

"Finn Bentley! From the first time I read your résumé I was intrigued with your scholastic record; then when I ordered and read your graduation speech I was in awe at the wisdom and sincerity with which you spoke. You are a find. It's not every day that someone with a generous spirit like yours comes along, and believe me when I say, I am and will be forever grateful."

"Thank you, Sam. There is, however, just one more thing I believe should be handled with the utmost expedience—actually two things. Devin needs to be updated about your condition to assure him that you are receiving proper care from Camilla and me. Next, there is the delicate matter of his adoption that would simultaneously need to be disclosed. Once everyone is on the same page, we can all proceed with a strong unified front ready to deal with any obstacles that might present themselves in the future. Devin is not a child anymore, but a full grown man, who I am sure can handle the truth with the resilience of a mature adult."

"All I can say is I am sure glad to know you are on my team," Sam said admiringly.

The alarm on my watch sounded and I was reminded of my meeting at the precinct. I asked Sam to excuse me and told him I had an appointment I needed to attend.

"Yes, of course. Thank you for our little chat."

CHAPTER 8

FIRST MEETING WITH LT. MYERSON.

When I got back to my desk, I had barely enough time to collect my things to take home before Devin appeared at the door and asked if I was ready to leave. His commitment and eagerness to watch over me afforded me a degree of assurance that I was not alone in my battle with this hidden attacker. Devin suggested we take my car and afterwards I would drive him back to the office garage where we could talk. Walking to the RAV4 in the parking lot felt a lot safer with him at my side. When we got to the station I told the officer at the desk who I was and reminded him of my appointment with LT. Myerson at five o'clock.

"Oh, yes! Mr. Bentley. The lieutenant is expecting you." Devin and I followed him into the inspector's office. As soon as we cleared the door, she looked up and shot me an amused smile.

"Mr. Bentley, I presume! I'm Sandra Myerson. By the look on your face I perceive you weren't expecting a female? Don't be embarrassed, I get that a lot."

"I'll admit I was caught off guard by the moniker above the door," I said smiling. "The title 'LT. Myerson, detective' did nothing to warn me of your gender. But once I give you the specifics of my problem I'm sure that you will realize that your being male or female does not matter to me in the least."

"Fine, Let's start with introducing your handsome friend here, and what he has to do with this."

"Yes, this is Devin Elkins, my boss's son and fellow associate at Bernard-Severson. It's an advertising firm on the seventeenth floor of the Butler Building downtown. When I confided in him about a possible stalker situation, Devin stepped up to the plate and volunteered to help guard me closely so as to keep me safe from being surprised by an unexpected assailant. He assures me he is a student of martial arts and can handle himself quite deftly should the circumstance arise."

"How do you do, Mr. Elkins?" she greeted him in a friendly tone.

"Fine! Thank you, and please just call me Devin."

"And you can call me Sandy."

"And while we're exchanging such pleasantries," I interjected amusingly, "you can call me Finn."

"Well now that we all know each other on a first name basis, what is it that brings you in here today? The note you left at the front desk said someone is being stalked. Let's start with who is being stalked."

Sandy looked to be about 40-ish, and very attractive with straight red hair, though nicely styled. She had green eyes that could look at you captivatingly. All in all she exhibited an air of being one who is in authority.

"I'm sure most of the stalking cases you deal with are females not males. I don't know if this has any bearing on my case or not, but I am gay—a fact that I would appreciate being kept quietly with your utmost discretion."

"That is unusual, but not out of the realm of possibility. I've worked at this desk for ten whole years now and believe me when I say I've seen it all. But rest assured, anything you tell me today will be kept in the strictest confidence. However, it may help if you give me a little more background about yourself."

"I figured it might be advantageous for you to know as much about me as possible so I brought you a copy of the résumé I submitted to Bernard-Severson. From it you can have an outline of my education and places of employment, as well as my residences for the last 19 years. My mother and I moved here to Philadelphia a year ago from Newton, PA. We live in the Bonnieville Arms, on Ridge Avenue."

"I'm familiar with that area; it's a very nice area, but go on."

"I recently gained employment with Bernard-Severson, and on Wednesday the 16th of this month, Mom and me went out shopping for clothes to wear at my new job. When we got back to the apartment parking garage, we let Jimmy, a 14-year-old junior high school boy, who has a side business carrying in people's packages, take our purchases up to our apartment. Mom and I had just boarded the elevator to go to the seventh floor when the elevator door started to close and I happened to turn and spy a suspicious person in a black hoodie looking at us from the far end of the garage. When he noticed he was seen, he conspicuously ducked behind one of the concrete pillars. The door closed, and Mom and I went up to our floor and I didn't think any more about it until the same person appeared again the next week."

"You say there was a second time. Were you able to identify the sex of this individual?" Sandy asked.

"Not at the first sighting, but at the second one I was sure he was a male."

"How can you be so sure it was a man?"

"I could tell by his walk. He started walking toward me menacingly and I'm sure he had a taser in his left hand. I still couldn't get an accurate look at his face since most of it was covered by the black hoodie. Luckily the executive elevator door opened and three employees stepped out on the garage floor. When he saw that there were too many witnesses to deal with, he beat a hasty retreat down the stairwell."

"If you are right about the taser, we can be reasonably certain he didn't mean to kill you. More than likely he meant to abduct you, which gives us something at least to go on. He would have to have had a vehicle close by in which to transport you once you were immobilized. We can request a tape of the footage from the security cameras on that level of the garage to see if there were any vehicles out of the ordinary there that day. Maybe we'll get lucky and even get a license plate. Just one more thing, Finn, do you have any idea who this might be that is stalking you?"

"No, Sandy! I've wracked my brain trying to come up with a name. For the past two years I've been living a very sheltered life. It's only recently I've come out from seclusion in a prison of my own making. If I come up with anything I'll let you know."

"Well, I think we've got enough to go on for now. Fill out this form with your contact information before you leave. Oh! And you may as well leave us Devin's info too. I'll get back to you as soon as we learn anything from the security cameras."

We stood, shook hands, and turned to leave. Devin was curiously silent through the whole meeting. It wasn't until we got outside that he became more vocal, like the Devin to which I was more accustomed. Sandy, on the other hand, I perceived was noticeably attracted to his good looks. She tried to hide it, but I caught her several times sneaking glances at him all during our intercourse.

As soon as we were outside in my car, the quiet Devin took hold of my arm, pulled me close, and kissed me long and desperately on the lips.

"I was terrified in there listening to you describe that account in the parking garage of the Butler Building, especially when you mentioned the part about him carrying a taser. Finn, this sicko wants to have you. Who is this lunatic? How and why has he made you his target? I'm not afraid of him, but I'm horrified to think what he has in mind to do to you if he ever succeeds in capturing you. We could be dealing with a serial killer."

"Maybe this last failed attempt discouraged him and he wont take it any further," I tried to assure him. "Let's wait and see what develops from here before we get too paranoid."

"Paranoid or not, when we get back to the garage I'm going to follow you home and see to it personally that you get through your front door safely."

"Well, if you're that determined, when we get to the apartment, you might as well come in and meet Mom. She's been wanting to meet you ever since I told her how handsome you are. My being lonely has been a constant concern of hers ever since Jake died. Once she meets you, and realizes how wonderful you are, maybe she'll settle down and not worry about me so much."

Changing the subject produced a calming effect on Devin's anxiety level. He chuckled at my description of him, and his face took on that charismatic smile that I found so irresistible. When we got to the parking garage, he got out of my car and entered his Mustang and followed me home to the Bonnieville Apartment building. On the way there I called ahead to warn her that I was bringing home a guest who would probably be staying to dinner.

"Don't worry about what we'll eat. I have a Cordon Bleu in the freezer that I've kept for emergencies. It can be thawed in the microwave quickly and the rest I can whip together in a flash." She wanted to know who it was I had invited, but all I said was, "It's a surprise!"

CHAPTER 9

GUESS WHO'S COMING TO DINNER?

Mom was at the door waiting anxiously when I turned the key to let in Devin and myself.

"Mother, this is Devin Elkins, the boss's son, the one I told you that I'd be working with."

It didn't take a Hollywood talent scout to notice that Mom was immediately taken with Devin's charming countenance as well as the rest of him that was equally pleasing. He had the same effect on every woman he and I had met so far.

As soon as we entered the living room she invited him to take a seat and offered him something to drink. Neither Mom nor I drank hard liquor although we would take a small glass of wine periodically.

"Can I get you a glass of water or some ice tea maybe?" Mom asked, sounding like a flight attendant.

"Yes some ice tea would be perfect, thank you!" Devin accepted, a little amused at her obvious fawning over him.

Swiftly I came to his rescue and began filling Mom in on the reason for our new visitor.

"Mom, I invited Devin here tonight for two reasons. One is because we are on the edge of becoming partners. I didn't think it could happen twice, but I've fallen in love with him, and I thought this would be a propitious time for us all to meet. Which brings me to my second reason for our meeting..."

Suddenly Devin looked up and shot me a shocked smile. He was surprised to hear me admit that my feelings toward him had progressed to such a desired level. He had fallen for me way back on that September night long ago when looking through the threshold of the cabin door our eyes first met and the wheels of destiny were mysteriously set in motion. Whereas for me, the awareness of our fateful joining together again wasn't awakened until that serendipitous reunion today at Mitzy's.

Then continuing on, I told Mom to take a seat on the sofa because we had something serious to talk about. She already knew about the two sightings of a stalker in the two separate garages, but she wasn't aware of my going to the police station, or my meeting with Lt. Sandra Myerson. She sat there quietly listening until I got to the part about the taser; then she reacted with the same alarm as Devin.

"That's too scary, Phineas! Whoever this person is, he's obviously after you for a reason. Do you have any idea who it might be or why he's after you?"

"No, Mom, Ms. Myerson asked me the same question. I gave her the same answer I'm giving you; I haven't got a clue."

"Just the same, Phineas. Too much protection is better than not enough."

Suddenly Devin broke in, "That's why I've committed myself to watching over him as much as possible. I'm afraid you may get sick of seeing my face around here until he's out of danger."

"No fear of either Mom or I getting tired of seeing too much of your handsome face," I assured him.

"Oh dear!" Mom exclaimed. "I almost forgot to tell you about the upcoming tour Avis has set up with the book club. They're going on a three-day bus trip up to New York City this weekend, but now in light of recent happenings I'd be afraid to leave you alone here in the apartment. It sounds like a good one too. It includes, among other interesting things, a Broadway musical, a tour of the Freedom Tower, Ellis Island, the Statue of Liberty, and three five-star restaurants."

The idea of being left by ourselves all weekend lit both our faces like a Christmas tree.

"Mom, don't you worry about things being safe here while you're away. I'm sure Devin and I are quite competent to protect each other."

Suddenly Mom innocently blurted out one of her trite tongue in cheek quips without even thinking, "You mean I'm leaving the fox to guard the henhouse."

At that we all broke into spontaneous laughter letting the word associations in our minds bind to their visual counterparts.

"Really, Mom, you need this trip. You've been holed up in this apartment way too long. Go and have a great time. Don't worry about us; we'll be fine."

Getting Mom active and growing in her new social life solved two problems. One, it helped her make friends and escape the boredom of being alone all day long. And two, it afforded the necessary space that Devin and I needed to get better acquainted intimately. Only one month ago I wouldn't have thought it possible, but now I found myself looking forward to it with great anticipation. My one regret was having to keep secrets from him. I longed to tell him about his heritage, but for now it was best leaving that to his father.

After dinner and Devin had left for his own apartment, Mom and I sat down to talk.

"Phineas, your young man is quite a catch. I can tell he's very taken with you, and I can see you feel the same way toward him. It's good to see you're going on with your life. Jake would be happy to know that you're no longer letting yourself be trapped in loneliness and self-pity. In a way, he even gave his approval that night you told him about Devin's impetuous kiss on the front porch."

"Yes," I added reminiscently. "When I told him about it and asked him not to get angry, he just laughed and said, 'How could I get angry with someone who sees in you the same treasure I see, and wanted to kiss you? It serves you right for being so damn cute.'"

"In the morning you should contact Bob the security guard," Mom suggested, "and alert him to what is happening. Also ask him to walk you to your car every morning starting tomorrow until this whole business goes away."

"I'm beginning to feel like a protected species, but when you consider the alternative, being abducted, and murdered, it's comforting to know help is close by if I need it."

CHAPTER 10

SECRETS AND THREATS

The next day the bell at the front door rang and I hurried to open it, but not before looking first through the peep hole to make sure who it was.

"Bob! You're a little early. Would you like to come in and have a cup of coffee?"

"Don't mind if I do, Finn," Bob answered with his usual cheerful greeting.

As soon as he was seated comfortably and I handed him his coffee, I began filling him in on only the details I felt were pertinent for him to know.

"Thanks for giving me the heads up about this, Finn, especially the thing about the taser. Those are nasty, and most criminals carry them these days. Things like that are less effective against a victim if the victim is aware of them. Like it says in Proverbs ,'In vain is the snare set in the sight of any watching bird.'"

Bob was one of those Christians that was always quoting the Bible. He knew about my being gay, but he never judged or condemned me for it, which was something for which I highly respected him. Having someone straight like him for a friend is a rare and valued thing with gay people. I would be more inclined to talk with him about his faith, when the time is right, than to open up about my personal life to someone who insists in coming at me with laws that condemn. I knew I could be myself around him; he was the most loving and patient man I had ever met.

"The plan, Bob, is to walk me to my car Monday through Friday morning unless I notify you ahead of time that I have it covered by my boyfriend."

"I'll be happy to do anything to keep you safe, Finn. After all, you and your mom are two of my favorite people in the whole building. You can always tell the people who have moved in from out of town; they're so much more friendly."

"That's a very nice compliment, Bob, but we'd better get moving so I can make it to work on time."

When I pulled into my parking space at the Butler Building, Devin was waiting for me in his parking space.

"I didn't want to take any chances on our friend showing up, so I decided to be here to escort you up to the office," Devin assured.

"Thank you, babe. I really appreciate your caring for me like this."

Suddenly it dawned on me that this was the first time I had used a term of affection for him instead of calling him by his first name. His facial expression conveyed his elation evidenced from the fact that our relationship was now reaching a more intimate level.

"Do you mind my calling you that?" I asked.

"Absolutely not. You never have to apologize to me for being affectionate. If I acted surprised, it's because I want you to know how happy it makes me to know that we are getting closer to each other," he said reassuringly, "and I don't ever want anything to change between us."

For me to believe that anyone as beautiful as him could love me seemed inconceivable. Yet here he was pledging his deepest affection to me and my heart being filled with an unbelievable joy. But my exhilaration was about to experience a chilling reduction when I got to my office and found two notes on my desk, one from Sam Elkins and the other from my stalker.

I read the one from Sam first: "Finn, please come and see me first thing."

The other note read: "I'm coming for you, and nothing, or no one can stop me. You're not my first. There have been others before you and no one could save them either. You shall be for my temporary pleasure, and when I'm through with you I will discard you like the rest. YOUR DESTINY."

If he meant this to scare me, he was sadly mistaken. I've known gay bashers in the past, even those who threatened me with bodily harm, and by now the impulse in me to fight back was stronger than the temptation to give in to fear. He was not going to ruin my day. If Sam wanted me first thing, then Sam would be first to have me.

I knocked on his door and entered when I heard his friendly inviting voice.

"Finn, I'm afraid our plan to have you take over for Camilla has been moved up. Camilla informed me that an emergency has happened with her sister and she will be leaving permanently at noon today. Which means your extra duty of babysitting me will begin at 3:00 to 4:00 today. I hope this sudden change doesn't spoil any plans you may have made previously."

"No, Sam! There are no other plans that would interfere with my aiding you today, and even if there were, I would happily cancel them; you are my first priority. But who are you going to use as a secretary to replace Camilla out in front?"

"Diane Benson from copy editing indicated to me she was interested in taken over the job when she heard Camilla was leaving. She'll be an adequate replacement and her secretarial skills are more than sufficient. The only foreseeable problem I can she is that she has a thing for Devin, which is obvious by the way she lights up every time she gets near him. He and I have talked about it in the past, and he assured me he is not in the least interested, a fact that is puzzling to me to me since she is a very beautiful woman."

Sam thankfully was not aware why I had covered my mouth with the palm of my right hand to keep from chuckling out loud. Women competitors are no threat to gay couples so I understood Devin's response totally. What was even more obvious was that Sam was not aware that his son and I had a history that went back a few years and had recently flared up again stronger than ever.

"What do you recommend I tell him if he asks me why I am spending an hour every day behind locked doors alone with you in your office? I mean, he knows I'm gay, and I would rather he knew the truth about what's going on in here than have him think the worst."

Sam broke in with, "I've been trying to buy some time to figure out how to tell him about his adoption and my epileptic seizures, but I keep drawing blanks."

"He and I have established a good rapport since we started working together. I'd be willing to do it for you," I said. "But I think he would rather it came from you than from me."

Suddenly Sam blind-sided me with a startling suggestion. "How about we both tell him at the same time?"

"How do you propose we do that?" I said somewhat baffled.

"We can call him in the office 3:30, sit him down, and I'll explain it all to him. I'd feel much more comfortable with you in the room. I'm not as reticent to tell him about my health condition as

I am about how to approach the subject of his adoption," Sam confessed.

"It sounds like a good plan, but now, if you'll excuse me, I must talk to him about another matter of importance. I'll bring him in here with me when I come back at 3:00."

The outer office door was a quicker route to Devin's desk so I approached his office space that way. When I got next to his chair I bent over and whispered in his ear, "Devin, honey! Come into my office, I have something important to show you."

He looked at me puzzled, but didn't question. He waited a few minutes after I was back in my office to avoid suspicion from any coworkers that might be watching, then came in through my front door. "Sit down. I need you to look at this note I found on my desk this morning." I handed him the piece of paper and studied his facial expression as he read it.

"This guy must be a psycho. We need to report this to Sandy right away."

"We'll go after hours today to see what she has to say about this. They're more experienced in dealing with these kind of perps."

"I agree with you, love, but today is not a good day to go to the station. You and I have a meeting with your father at 3:30 in his office. I'll give her a call and fax her a copy of the note as soon as you return to your desk."

"A meeting?" he responded perplexed.

"Yes, and that's all I can tell you for now, so please don't try to pressure it out of me. I'm sworn to secrecy. But believe me, before this day is over, everything will be cleared up and it will be a great weight off my shoulders. Do you think you can grant me one big favor though?"

"Sure, anything you want. Name it!" he complied. "I'm happy for the chance to be the chosen source of your pleasure."

"With all that's going on right now, I would consider it a pleasant diversion if you would take me to Taco Bell for lunch today."

"Agreed!" he said. With a knowing grin. "Although from now until 3:30 I'll be wrapped up in suspense about this meeting."

"Okay. Let's call Lt. Myerson and update her on this latest development in the case." I pulled her card out of my wallet and dialed the number of her cell phone."

"Hello! Lt. Myerson," her voice came over her cell.

"Hi, Sandy! It's Finn Bentley. There's been a new development in my case. I received a threatening note when I got to my desk this morning. I'm going to fax a copy to you."

"By all means send me a copy, but we're also going to need the original here to dust it for fingerprints. Is there any way you can get it to us today? What format is it in? Is it handwritten or typed?"

"No it's the old unoriginal way with the words cut out of newspaper clippings; it seems our man has a flare for drama."

"Still we can dust it for prints, although I don't have much hope we will find any. These guys usually take all the precautions needed to remain unknown. I'll send a man over to pick it up this afternoon. Put it in a sealed manila envelope and write 'Attention, LT. Sandra Myerson' on it. We'll talk again tomorrow. I should have more info on the garage camera footage to show you by then."

"Will do. Talk to you later, Sandy."

Devin and I chose to eat our lunches on the outside tables at Taco Bell. It was my first time eating TB's food since before Jake died. The pig inside me devoured two tacos and a chalupa shamelessly, and washed it down with a large Diet Coke. To keep Devin's mind off the coming afternoon meeting, I introduced a different topic into the conversation.

"I hate having to be secretive about our relationship," I said. "But for now it is the wisest thing to do."

"I know what you mean and I am in total agreement with you," Devin added. "Once we get all this intrigue out of the way, and this perp is caught, I want to take you on a cruise where we can be free to express ourselves away from the scrutiny of meddlesome people who feel they need to be our judges."

"When did you first realize you were gay?" I asked.

Devin looked straight into my eyes, and his expression turned serious. "I guess I knew it from a very early age, though at first I didn't want to accept it so I tried to deny it by convincing myself that I might be bi-sexual. That made life a little easier, but never entirely satisfactory. There were many years of having to endure loneliness and the secret need for male tenderness. Then there was the constant temptation to ignore all the danger signs and recklessly indulge my curiosity by exploring forbidden territory. Loneliness is a powerful force to reckon. Straight or gay, sooner or later, all of us have to face the fact that down deep inside is an empty void that must be filled. No one is exempt from the power covertly lurking deep inside each of us. My greatest horror would be to die without it ever being assuaged, if only for a short while. When I first saw you I knew you were the one who could save me from a life ending in regret. Even having to live with only a torturous hope was better than being bullied with the constant threat of living with no love at all. That is why, my love, ever since we came together again, I haven't been able to focus on anything except holding you in my arms and making love to you."

"Obviously your years of suffering were not without due compensation," I commented. "You've gained valuable insight during that painful period of introspection."

Slowly, I was realizing that Devin was not the shallow, nepotistic co-worker I had originally envisioned. The level of maturity he had reached was clearly through his own independent achievement, and he deserved whatever position in the company that his dad had placed under his supervision. He had the rare ability to think through life's complexities and stay resilient enough not to allow them to destroy him. I was counting on this level of maturity when His father and I talked to him later in today's meeting. The depth of character in him was drawing me irresistibly into his allure. Once I was like a fortress unconquerable, now I was a city being overthrown and begging for terms of surrender. A gentle transfer of ownership in my heart had taken over. In the place where Jake had once occupied, now Devin had moved in and the truth of my love for him was becoming unshakable.

"We need to get back to the office," I said finally. "We've got that meeting with your father, and I have to get that manila envelope on the secretaries desk before the policeman gets there."

CHAPTER 11

SPILLING THE ADOPTION

At exactly 3:30 p.m. Devin walked into his Dad's office and the door was locked behind him. Sam bade us to sit on the sofa. We sat on opposite ends to maintain discretion of our secret relationship. Then he moved around from his desk to the overstuffed chair adjacent to us, and while facing us squarely he launched without delay into his dialogue.

"Devin, this meeting is mainly for your benefit. I've asked Finn to sit in and aid me in case I leave out any important details that you may need to know. There are two imperative issues you will need to be made aware of today."

Devin sat in guarded silence, not knowing what to expect. His full attention directed toward his father, as Sam continued his explanation for the meeting.

"My health has deteriorated over the past two years, Devin. Nothing critical, mind you, but at least something requiring personal assistance. About a year and a half ago, I began suffering epileptic seizures, which required someone to be on hand whenever they occurred. In the past Camilla had been helping me, but when it became necessary for her to leave our employ, I asked Finn to step in and take over my care after Camilla's departure. Finn has graciously accepted the task of caring for me. He explained that you should be made privy to all this in case you wondered why he was spending one hour every day alone with me in my office behind locked doors. We both agreed that you should know the truth as a fail-safe so that you would not think the worst—a false but completely logical assumption. You recall, that since I decided that you and he would be working together, I thought it best to allow you to read his confidential résumé so you'd know about his gender preferences.

Devin shot an embarrassing smirk at me then quickly removed it from his face. I could see he found the circumstance amusing, but this was not the time for levity.

"Finn brought up another dilemma," Sam continued. "We

needed to clear up for you the question of whether or not my condition is hereditary. The truth is that that question is moot. There is something I've needed to talk to you about for a long time but hoped it would be a topic that would never have to be approached."

Before he could continue, Devin broke in and explained, "If it's about my being adopted, we don't need to labor through it, Dad. I've known about that since I was sixteen."

The look of surprise that swept over Sam's face was like someone struck dumbfounded.

"What, what! How did you ever find out about your adoption?" Sam asked in shock.

"When I was 16, Dad, you and Mother went to Hawaii for your eighteenth wedding anniversary. While you were gone I needed to find a gun permit that was signed by you as my parent or guardian. It was in a box of important papers on the top shelf in your bedroom closet. I apologize now for rummaging through your stuff before first asking your permission, but I didn't want to bother the two of you on your vacation. But when I was shuffling through your papers, my eyes spied my birth certificate. The names of my true biological parents were there. I ran to my bedroom, got my camera, and came back to take a picture of the document. All during the remainder of that week that you were gone, I researched my real parents names through reels of old newspapers on microfilm at the city library and found out about their demise on United flight 93 on 9/11. I decided never to tell you and Mom what I knew unless you brought it up first."

Sam sat there listening speechless, tears started running down his cheeks. Seeing a manly figure like him cry brought sympathetic tears to my eyes as well.

"I want you to know, son, that there was never a day that went by that your mother and I didn't love you and think of you as our own. When we received news of that plane crash, we took it as a sign from God that we three had saved each other. You saved us from a life of facing childless years ahead, and we believe that if we hadn't taken you, you might have been on that plane with your real parents when it went down. Our union was surely a gift from God."

"Ever since I found out the fate of my real parents," Devin said, choking back tears of gratitude, "I have realized how fortunate I was to be placed in the care of two such wonderful people like you and Mother. I love you, Father, and you will always be to me my true dad."

After the meeting ended and Devin and I were both back in my office, we agreed to hold off telling Sam about the delicate matter with the stalker until a later date. Then also there was that little tidbit of Devin coming out to him about being gay. And the other shocker of our being lovers. Although we felt he had the right to know, today was not a convenient time to approach topics with possible explosive repercussions. The two landmark topics that came out of today's meeting presented the three of us with enough capricious discoveries to absorb during one 24-hour period.

Just then my cellphone rang and the display read Sandy Myerson on it. I answered, "Hi, Sandy, this is Finn!"

"Hello, Finn, I'm so glad I caught you before you left for home. Will you and Devin be able to come down to the station for a short meeting tomorrow afternoon? There's been some interesting developments in your case of which we feel you need to be made aware."

"Sure, Sandy, we can be there about 4:30."

"Perfect! See you then," she said and hung up.

"Hon! Sandy said she had some important new information to give us. Would you be willing to come with me to the station tomorrow after work?" I pleaded.

"Absolutely! I'm with you all the way with this thing," Devin said with a reassuring tone.

"I'm so glad you're standing with me babe. I don't know what I'd do if I had to face this mess alone," I said, quivering.

It was quitting time, and Devin walked me to my car and followed me home before heading back to his place. Mom and I spent a placid evening at home, just the two of us. Somehow I couldn't shake the feeling that it was the calm before the storm. All hell was about to break loose, and my intuition was sending me warning signals to get ready.

CHAPTER 12

NARROWING THINGS DOWN

By the time Thursday rolled around we were thankful there were no more solicitations on the client list until Friday. Everything at the office was running smoothly and we were able to catch up on all our paper work.

We waited until four o'clock to insure Sam would be free from suffering an episode. Then Devin and I jumped in my car and drove to the downtown police station. The officer on duty escorted us into the office of Lt. Sandy Myerson who was waiting and prepared to go into action as soon as we got there.

"Hi, Finn! And, Devin, I'm glad you could make it as well. Take a seat and I'll show you what we've been able to find out so far about your stalker. First of all we dusted the note for fingerprints and came up empty there. No surprise, they never do leave fingerprints on notes like that. Of course, since it wasn't handwritten but just all newspaper clippings, we couldn't match it with our handwriting experts either. But our efforts weren't a total loss, and this is where the bad news comes in. We were able to examine sentence structure and word usage and found a match with notes that were sent to some other gay men like you who were later abducted and murdered in two other neighboring states—Pennsylvania; Delaware, and Maryland. Because the crimes crossed state lines, the FBI have now entered into the investigation, and with them and us working together, we have hopes of catching the perp soon."

"This is getting more and more dangerous all the time," Devin said, revealing a gradual loss of trust.

"Yes, but we now know more about him than we did before," Sandy said, trying to restore his confidence.

"What about the camera footage in the parking garage you were going to check out?" I said.

"We were given complete cooperation from the owners of the Butler Building, but the surveillance footage turned out nothing helpful so far. Your attacker wore a black hoodie and we couldn't get any worthwhile facial recognition. As for a vehicle parked on that floor that didn't belong, we drew a blank on that also. He must have had his car parked on another level. Our guess is that his plan was to drag you into the hallway after you were tasered and then drive his vehicle around to pick you up later. Unfortunately, that is all we have to go on so far."

"Now, Finn, have you been able to come up with a name of anyone whom you might suspect would want to do you harm?" Sandy queried. "Has anyone ever assaulted you at any time?"

"There was this boy in school who propositioned me, and when I refused his advances he slapped me. My boyfriend caught him striking me and punched him hard enough in the face to knock him down. His name was Thomas Grogan and he had transferred to Newton High School from Maryland. The school principal expelled him, and he was told he would not ever be welcomed back."

Before I could even finish giving her the info on Tom, Sandy was already busy searching her computer for his name on the police national crime list.

"Yes, here it is. Thomas Grogan. After being expelled from Newton High School, Mr. Grogan's record got worse. He was arrested for a string of burglaries and petty thefts, until finally he was convicted for the crime of statutory rape of a 13-year-old girl. He was sent to Maryland State Prison where he is currently serving a 15-year term without the possibility of parole. Well, I guess that rules him out since he's got the perfect alibi. How about we put our heads together and see if we can come up with someone else? Let's see, your first sighting was at your apartment building garage after your job interview and before your first day at work with Bernard-Severson, is that correct?"

"Yes, Sandy, that is correct," I offered, in hopes of being helpful.

"Then if your stalker is not connected with your previous life then we can assume he is somehow connected with your job at Bernard-Severson. It's quite likely you have rubbed shoulders with this guy since you started your duties last Monday. Can you think of anyone that you've gotten suspicious vibes from recently?"

"It's strange that you should use that particular phrase Sandy. About 'rubbing shoulders' I mean. I did have a strange encounter with a man who works for our company. It didn't happen my first day of work though; it happened a week ago Wednesday, the day I came in for an interview. After Sam agreed to hire me and I was leaving the office, Ms. Vandervere called the maintenance man Alex over and asked him to show me to my reserved parking space. He showed me to the private elevator that accesses the employee parking. Then as we were entering the cage he deliberately rubbed his shoulder against mine. When I gave him a puzzled look he offered no explanation. He had a sly smile on his face that made me suspect he knew my secret, but how could he. Only my boss Sam and I knew I was gay and I have complete trust in his confidence. How could Alex have guessed it?"

As I was relating this story, I noticed by the look on Devin's face that he was listening keenly and his countenance grew suspicious.

"I think I can answer that!" said Devin.

Sandy and I both shot him a questioning look.

"If Alex is indeed our man, he could very easily have gained access to all the information he needed to know about Finn. His hours of work at the building are usually 10 a.m. to 6 p.m., except on Fridays when he cleans all the offices and cubicles. On that day only, he comes in at 12:00 and leaves around 8 p.m., which would give him ample time to spy through any private information filed in anyone's office cabinets. It's quite possible he read the résumé you submitted with your application Finn, and the transcript from your valedictorian speech that Dad ordered from Newton High School. He would have learned you are gay and from that point on you became a target for his rage. That also explains how he first turned up at your residence parking lot on that Thursday after your interview and Fad hired you."

Devin is a quick mover once he decides to proceed with a course of action in which he is certain. All the while he was talking to us, he was texting personnel at the office to send a copy of Alex Wilkes's job application to Sandy's fax number from her business card.

"If your suspicions are correct, Devin," Sandy said, "I'm going to need all the information you have on this Alex as soon as you can get it to me."

"It's already done. If you'll check your fax machine, you'll find it's all there."

Sandy first looked over at the fax machine then back to Devin with an amazed expression.

"There's just one more thing before you go, Finn. Is there anything unusual about Alex that you noticed that might help us with his arrest?

"When we were getting into the elevator I noticed an ugly burn mark on his forearm, just above his right wrist. When I commented on it to him, he said it happened while barbecuing in his back-yard."

"Thanks, that could be important, but we'll have to wait to find out. It's all here," she said. "Why don't you two go home and let us take it from here. There is one precaution; carry on as if nothing unusual is afoot. We don't want this Alex to know we're on to him."

Devin and I were ready to call it quits anyway after such a long and emotionally draining day. I called ahead and told Mom we were coming home and that Devin would be staying the night. On the way home, we drove to Devin's house and packed a light suit-case so he and I would be able to leave for work from the Bonnie-ville Apartments in the morning. We decided it would be more strategic to leave his car at the Butler parking garage and to pool using mine for the present.

CHAPTER 13

INTIMACY DEFERRED

"Hi, Mom! I'm home!" I shouted, as Devin and I walked through the door.

"Hi, sweetheart," Mom yelled from her bedroom. "I'll be out in a minute as soon as I finish packing. Have you given any thought to dinner or shall we order from Cavacinni's?"

"If you don't mind, I've got a manicotti in the freezer and breadsticks to go with it," I yelled back. "I'll whip up a nice green salad with tomatoes, olive oil, and vinaigrette dressing. There's a nice bottle of red wine in the pantry also."

"Hi, handsome!" Mom shot her friendliest compliment at Devin when she made her entrance to the living room."

"Hi, Mrs. Bentley," Devin returned.

"Just call me Donna," Mom said. "I've got a feeling you're going to be hanging around here for a while so you may as well make yourself a familial part of the furniture."

"Thanks, Donna, I appreciate that."

"Phineas, you remember what tomorrow is, don't you?"

"Yes!" I said. "It's Friday." Feigning a loss of memory about her trip to NYC. I wanted her to feel like every thought about this club and its activities were the product of her own decision making. If she got wind that I was manipulating her, any future endeavors on my part would be severely compromised.

"Tomorrow my club leaves for or tour of New York. Us girls will be leaving here to board the bus at five in the morning. It'll be parked outside in front of the apartment building. We are paying Roger a little extra to come in early and help us load our suitcases on the bus. Don't worry about you and Devin having to get up. Roger will be outside our door with the luggage rack, and he's got everything covered."

"Sounds good, Mom. I'm glad you reminded us. I hope you and the rest of the girls have lots of fun. And don't worry about Devin and I here. I'll be safely taken care of by the security guard, and no one would dare try anything with my strong man here to keep me safe," I said, with a degree of levity to relieve any tension she might be having. "Now let's sit down and have a nice relaxing dinner before you go to bed. You're going to need to build up some reserve before tomorrow's trip."

After dinner, Mom retired to her bedroom. Devin and I sat down on the sofa and had a nice long talk before getting up and walking into the bedroom in anticipation of our first lengthy time alone together.

Just like with Jake, Devin and I shared the bed naked. I undressed first and crawled into bed while Devin sat in the chair facing me next to the bed. He looked at my body, defenseless and unadorned, like a man eyeing a treasure he had searched for all his life. Now he had finally acquired someone he could call his own.

"Finn, that first glimpse I got of you that September at the cabin, I knew I wanted you and I would never be able to settle for anyone else but you. It was love at first sight. I fell for you then and I loved you from that moment on. That stolen kiss at Christmas I shared with you was an act out of sheer desperation. Our lips were only able to make contact for a few seconds, but in that short time I wanted our souls to bond in a way that you would never forget."

"Devin stood up and began disrobing. He was still clothed in his office suit with a shirt and tie. He removed his jacket first and walked over to my closet and hung it on a hanger. Next he removed his tie and wrapped it around the hanger with his jacket. He kept watching me with a serious expression as he slowly unbuttoned his shirt and folded it over the chair. Although I had never stepped foot into one of those clubs, the image of a male stripper was playing covertly in my mind. This was the first time I had seen his bare torso, having only been able to imagine his manly lines as seen through his office wardrobe. No wonder the girls were throwing themselves at him. His body development was superb in every way. It was obvious during his workouts at the gym that he spared no resistance to the muscles of his chest, arms, and abs. I sat up in bed watching this beautiful specimen of a man undressing, my heart pounding with each stitch of clothes he removed. Then he kicked off his shoes, unbuckled his belt, unzipped his pants and slid them slowly down and off on the floor, leaving only his black tight-fit boxer briefs. My eyes grew wide as he pulled them partially down and let them drop the rest of the way. Trying not to be obvious I couldn't help but gasp. Devin was what people called blessed in the size category of his genitals. I threw back the sheets and the comforter and invited him into my bed for the first time. He climbed in beside me and pulled me into his arms and began kissing me gently at first, letting me get use to the company of his strong masculine arms.

"Please, Devin, could we go slow tonight while Mom is still here in her room?" I whispered.

"Sure!" Devin assented. "I've waited all these years to have you, my love. We can wait one more night, though it won't be easy."

"Thank you, Devin, for being so understanding. I promise you tomorrow that you can have all of me and I will from then on hold nothing back. For tonight please just hold me in your arms and tell me that you love me."

Devin seemed to know what I wanted. He pulled me close to him in his arms and began kissing me first on the lips then on my neck and all around my upper body while deliberately avoiding the more erotic zones for the present in order to respect my wishes not to trespass my weaker defenses until later permitted. He was as much a gentleman as he was a genuine courtier. I lay there marveling that this gorgeous man was here for me, and for the present I was able to forget I was a misfit. I was unafraid to let go and love somebody who actually felt the same way about me.

We woke up the next morning in each other's arms, or rather I woke up in his arms? Mom had left early for New York with the ladies of her book club. It was the last day of the work week and Devin and I had one last scheduled visit with a prospective client. I let him snooze a few more minutes while I took a quick shower and started cooking a nice healthy breakfast to feed my hungry boy. He was just finishing up on his showering and shaving, putting on his suit and tie, and splashing on some intoxicating cologne, when I called him into the breakfast nook to sit down to eat. He raved about how wonderful the breakfast smelled and tasted, but all I could concentrate on was the scent of the manly cologne he was wearing.

Later in the car on the way to work I thanked him for being patient about last night's love making.

"That's okay," he said. "Anticipating tonight will make it that much more pleasurable."

"You can bet on it. I promise you it will be worth the wait and I always keep my promises."

CHAPTER 14

FRIDAY AND THE GATHERING STORM

We got to work at 10:00. The workroom was already busy with employees finishing up their work week in expectation of their personal activities planned for the weekend. Sam was occupied with his work, and Diane Benson was sitting at the receptionist desk at the front door of his office. When she saw Devin enter the room she shot him a sexy smile. Devin returned the smile but with an obvious message of his being noncommittal. I wondered what might be going through her head, when she noticed the two of us leaving together last night, and arriving back together this morning.

"Devin, do you think today might be a suitable time to come out to your father about our relationship? That is, of course if you feel secure about him being able to accept the fact of having a gay son. I'm willing to support your decision to go ahead today, or wait for a more prodigious time. I love you and would never force you into doing anything you were not ready to do."

"You need not feel like you are forcing me into anything, my love," Devin said in a comforting tone. "The truth is that I've been thinking about approaching Dad on the subject of my sexuality for quite some time. Today would be as good a time as any. When you go into his office today, between 3:00 and 4:00, I could come in whenever you think the time is right and we could lay all our cards on the table at once. Dad thinks very highly of you and that may weigh heavily to our advantage."

"Sounds like a good plan," I agreed. "Have you wondered at all how much easier our lives would be if I were born a genuine woman instead of being born gay?" I posed. "Heterosexuals don't have all the scrutiny to have to tolerate every day of their lives."

"They have their own set of troubles," Devin added. "None of us comes into this world immune to adversity. We all are delegated our share of rainy days to walk through. The key is to carry an umbrella for protection from the storm," he said with a smile. "With us, Finn, our love will be the umbrella to shelter us from all outside influences. Ever since you came back into these arms, you brought new life and meaning into my existence. I would not want to change one thing. You and I are going on together, Finn. Come hell or high water, we will face all the difficulties of life, and stand against the tide of negative public opinion, together. As long as we have love and each other, it will be more than enough to compensate for any temporal persecutions that life may throw our way."

"Well enough of philosophizing," I said. "Have you got a strategy in place for our meeting today with the client?" I asked.

"Yes! I do! But more about that when we leave at 11:00. I'll fill you in on the details in the car during the ride over to the plant."

CHAPTER 15

THE SURPRISE PROPOSITION

Eleven o'clock found Devin and I making our way to the elevator that empties on the executive floor of the parking garage. Although we took my Toyota, I insisted that Devin drive—a personal custom left over from my days with Jake. Once inside the car, I queried Devin about the client and the company we hoped to be representing.

"Client's name is John Welch and the company name is Welch industries.

They are one of the leading manufacturers of sporting goods in the country. They make all types of fishing and game equipment as well as their own rifle called The Predator which is on its way to being the most popular hunting rifle in today's market."

"Sounds impressive," I commented.

"I've only had one brief encounter with him last spring when he came to give a talk at Banner's college on the benefits of using the right equipment for the right job. He's definitely a man's man, if you know what I mean, which is why I think it best if I do most of the talking."

"Well I will readily concede that you are the more masculine one of the two of us."

"More masculine one?" Devin quipped.

"We'll alright, masculine one," I conceded.

We started laughing and after all the pressure and stress we had been under recently, it felt great to enjoy a little comic relief together.

… … … …

Mr. Welch's secretary led us into his office, told us to take a seat and that he would be with us shortly. Devin was right on point about him being a man's man. Every wall of his office was taken up by his mounted hunting and fishing trophies along with photos taken of him with famous men of government and military status. Just looking at all this manly furniture intimidated me and left me wishing that Devin had not brought me along today and had instead come alone.

Nevertheless, it was too late to cut and run. Through the door walked a tall, handsome, muscular John Welch with a big, warm, and friendly smile and an outstretched hand to greet us. I let Devin do the introductions while I was glad to accept the safer role of being a passive assistant. Curiously, when he took my hand to shake it, he sandwiched it between two of his and squeezed it at the same time drawing me closer to him. Immediately I became uncomfortably suspicious as to why he was using this non-verbal body language so soon in our initial meeting. Did he deduce I was gay right off and now was setting me up to expose me? What is it that people discover about me at a glance? Just when I think I have confidently disguised myself as a normal person, someone sees through my ruse and uncovers my true identity on first contact. But while my confidence was being stripped away, it was evident John's was planted firmly on solid ground. He looked at Devin, and before he could say a word, John suggested he first take a tour through the plant before talking business. Devin prudently decided to yield to John's take charge manner and glanced my way for me to accompany him.

"I've called for a tour guide to show you through the factory, Devin," John quickly intervened. "Mr. Bentley and I will remain here until you get back. Take your time and check us out carefully."

Devin looked at me questioningly as if to ask would I be alright by myself. I just looked back at him and shrugged my shoulders.

The tour guide arrived promptly and after John's brief introduction escorted Devin from the room. A feeling of apprehension swept over me. Alarming thoughts were playing havoc inside my brain. What was John's obvious private agenda? From my seat across the room, I looked him straight in the eyes but remained silent, waiting for him to speak first and reveal his hidden purposes. He took the seat behind his desk and began with a line of personal questions that at first made me very uneasy, but as his queries continued I become more and more self-composed.

"I wanted to talk with you privately Finn, that's why I asked you to stay behind so that certain aspects of our conversation could remain confidential. If you don't mind I'd like to ask you a personal question, and feel free to tell me to mind my own business or even tell me to go to hell. But if you do chose to answer, I am going to insist you answer it candidly and truthfully. If you and Devin Elkins want this account, be it known right up front, I don't want any bullshit. I value honesty above all else. So having said that, do I have your permission to proceed?"

There was a lot depending on my answers—that was evident from the earnest look in John's eyes. My mind was already settled on being upfront and my intuition was telling me that John would only accept my being totally transparent. With this course firmly imbedded in my psyche, I began my cautious reply.

"John, please feel free to ask me anything you want and I will answer it by being truthful. First to myself, and secondly to you."

"Okay, here goes. Finn Bentley, are you gay?"

Wow! I thought. John really cuts to the quick. Here's a man who doesn't believe in wasting time on subterfuge. My mind flashed back to the day when I first told Mom that Bernard-Severson had asked me to come in for an interview. She asked me then if I was going to tell them I was gay. My reply to her was still lucid in my memory. "Not unless it comes up. I prefer to keep it private, but I am not going to hide it either if they inquire." Yes, I am still of the same opinion I was then. My estimation of myself remains undaunted. I am not ashamed of it; it's what I am, and like William Shakespeare wrote in one of his plays, "To thine own self be true."

My eyes looked directly into his and I gave him my unequivocal answer.

"Yes. But I hope that won't influence your decision to use Bernard-Seversen's very successful marketing strategies for your sporting goods. In fact, I would consider quitting my job first if it meant that my being gay would in any way damage the companies reputation or encumber it's success."

"Relax, Finn!" John interrupted, as he hushed my zealous speech into silence. "Whether you're gay or not gay is not the main issue with me. My biggest priority is honesty, which you have so bravely proven to me by your display of faithfulness and candor. Your refusal to lie to cover up the fact of your gender difference was in itself sufficiently honorable, but you were even willing to sacrifice your job if need be to secure my account.

"Now let me assess all this, Finn: You're gay, you're damn cute, in fact you're exactly the kind of boy a man would like to take home with him tonight. Would you be open for some fun sometime if a guy were to ask?"

"John! I'm sure that most gay guys would jump at the chance to accept an offer like that from such a handsome, masculine man as you. But I am a one-man person. It's not that I don't love sex, I do, but I value love and commitment over mutual exploitation. I need love, John, I crave it, and I'm willing to wait for it, even if it means passing up a night of temporary pleasure with a man as beautiful as you."

John sat there staring at me with mixed feelings of hope and respect in his eyes. When he spoke it was out of words of sincere admiration.

"Finn, you are a person of exceptionally rare character. When Devin gets back from the diversion I sent him on, you can tell him you both can leave now. My lawyers read over the contract papers that you sent me earlier this week. They were signed and ready to go when you came through the door today. That is depending on how my meeting went today with you and him. I only have one more question to ask, but I fear the answer will not be to my liking."

He certainly knows how to put pressure on a guy, I thought silently to myself, as I awaited his last bit of probing, and hoped my answer wouldn't blow the whole deal. He walked over to my chair and reaching out with strong arms he lifted me to my feet, holding me close. Then looking squarely into my eyes, he asked softly, "Are you and Devin an item?"

My brain shifted into a fast thinking mode as it grasped for the right answer to appease his query. Why was he interested in Devin's and my relationship? At last I decided that the best answer to give him was the truth.

"Yes!" I admitted. "Devin and I are lovers and will always be lovers."

"Well if anything ever happens to change that, please let me be the first to know. I want to be there to pick up the pieces."

My reply had barely gotten out of my mouth when Devin returned from his tour. I walked over to him and said, "We can go now. I've got the papers all signed and we are done here." I started pulling him toward the door.

He turned and looked back at John questioningly, and said, "Are you sure you're not going to need me for anything."

"Nope, it's all over," John hollered back. "By the way, Devin, you are a lucky guy."

Those were the last words spoken to us by John Welch as Devin and I made our way to the parking lot and drove to lunch in silence. Lunch today called for a change of pace so we went to the Olive Garden.

CHAPTER 16

TIME TO GET REAL

No sooner had the host seated us at our table when Devin could hold back his curiosity no longer.

… … … …

"Okay! What happened back there? What did you say to him that made him like putty in your hands? How did you close the deal so quickly? And what was that last comment all about when he called me a lucky guy?"

"It seems your man's man is interested in more than just hunting big game. He picked up on the fact of my being gay as soon as he entered the office and saw me sitting there. From that time on he slipped into hunter/hunted mode and I became his prey. The first thing he needed to do was to get you out of the picture, so he sent you on a reconnaissance of the building with a tour guide to ensure your absence for a while and have time with me alone.

"You're kidding me?" Devin said, shocked. "John Welch, the man's man is a closet homosexual, or at the very least, a bi-sexual? That's a bit of knowledge he would not want to get around. I'm sure you and I agree we must keep it in our strictest confidence."

"Of course," I said. "We can both appreciate the benefits of discretion and/or the necessity of secrecy on the subject."

"Besides, we are going to have to deal with our own exposure with Dad later on today. Also we should check in with Sandy and see if there are any new developments in the case," I reminded. "We'll be back in the office by 1:00. Since today is Friday, Alex should have clocked in at 12:00. I wonder what new info Sandy was able to get on him. I'm curious as to what she found out about that burn mark on his forearm. When I think that we've worked in close proximity to a vicious serial killer all this time, it gives me the shivers. I'll be happy when we get back home tonight and crawl under the safety of the bed covers. I want you to make love to me so passionately that all the thoughts of this whole mess are completely pushed out of my head."

My favorite Italian dish is eggplant parmigiana. Devin had never had it so he decided to take a chance and order it also, and to his surprise he liked it. Since we had so much on our work plate, we hurried through lunch and headed back to the office.

We were a little late getting back at our desks, and it was 1:15 when we finally sat down to begin our afternoon duties. Devin thought it best to keep a close eye on Alex's activities so he called the personnel officer to check on his schedule.

… … … …

Margo, the personnel manager, answered the phone and checked the day's attendance list.

"No, Devin. Alex was supposed to be in at 12:00 but so far is a no call/no show." Devin thanked her and hung up.

Just then my cell phone rang; it was Sandy on the line.

"Good afternoon, Finn, it's Sandy from the bureau. Just to give you a heads up, we are coming there to arrest Alex and should be there shortly."

"Don't bother, he's not here," I countered. "He didn't show up for work today."

"I'll bet he caught wind that were on to him and is reassessing his plan of attack," Sandy said. "We'll put out an APB on him. We'll catch him. Don't worry. But until we do, you should realize that now since we don't know his whereabouts, that makes him all the more dangerous and you should be extra cautious whenever your outside. My experience with people like him is that even though he is on the run, finishing up with his last target here will be his highest priority."

"Meaning me, I presume." Finishing Sandy's thought.

"Exactly! You and Devin have both become targets, since we can assume that he has by now figured out that you are partners. If you notice anything suspicious, let us know immediately. Now that we're onto his game, time is on our side, and I'd like to keep it that way. As an extra precaution I'm sending a couple of plain clothes officers over there to keep a closer eye on you two. Officers Waddell and Randal will be staked out on the executive floor in the parking garage. They won't come up into your office unless, of course, you call them. By the way, you may be interested in one little detail we discovered about the burn mark on his arm. The previous boy he abducted and tasered was being transported in the front seat of his car with him. The kid was lucky enough to come to consciousness and pushed in the cigarette lighter without him noticing. When it heated up, he pulled it out and touched it to his Alex's right arm, above the wrist. Alex swore and stopped the vehicle long enough for the kid to exit and run away to safety. We now have the kids description and willingness to testify in court when it becomes necessary to go to trial.

After saying goodbye to Sandy, Devin and I finished up the paperwork from Welch Industries, and filed it in the cabinet under the heading of new business.

That makes two new accounts in two days we've brought into the company. Not bad for our first week," said Devin. "We make a great team."

"Let's hope our good record for success continues to hold out when we visit your dad later today. Which by the way it's almost 3:00 and I should be going into his office soon. I'll call you in at about four o'clock and we can enlighten him about both your gender preference and our romantic attachment at the same time."

After I made my way back to my desk, I finished up my paper reports of the past two days and knocked on Sam's door to signal I was about to enter for my hour of care giving. Sam had set the rules of what I could do or not do during my hourly watch.

"Come in, Finn, it's always a pleasure spending time with you." Sam was his usual cheerful self today which I hoped would continue as the afternoon unfolded.

"Anything exciting going on in your life? I hope you're not getting bored with the job. Are you and Devin getting along okay so far?"

"Oh yes! Devin and I are getting along famously."

I mused at the thought of the impending blockbuster news he was soon to be confronted with before the day was over.

"Well, as I told you. You may relax and do any activity of your own choosing during this hour. Most of all I want you to make an otherwise tedious duty as rewarding as possible so you won't consider it a burden."

"Sam, you may put that thought to rest. Since day one, at our first meeting, I have considered you to be the most honorable man I have ever met. I never had the fortune to know what having a dad was like because mine died when I was just two years old, but I can imagine that if I had one, while growing up, I would have considered myself very blessed if he had been just like you. And as far as this hour goes, being in here with you is actually the high point of my day. Whether we sit here and talk for the hour or just work side by side doing our separate projects, I would find our association just as fulfilling."

Sam's heart had grown very tender since his wife's death, and I could tell that my words had touched a soft spot deep inside him. He looked at me with watery eyes and told me how much he valued hearing me voice my appreciation. The end of the week posed some desk work for him too, so we both became silent during the rest of the hour. When time was approaching four o'clock, and it was clear Sam had passed the danger point of having an episode, I broke the silence and requested that he listen to something that Devin and I had to talk with him about.

"Why certainly, call him in and we can talk about it now."

After I called Devin into his dad's office and we took our seats side by side on the sofa, Sam moved from his desk and situated himself in the overstuffed chair facing us.

"I hope you two are happy with the present arrangement of working together," he opened with. "You're not unhappy are you?"

"Oh no! Quite to the contrary, Dad. Finn and I are very content working side by side as associates. My reason for wanting to talk with you today is about another subject that I've kept hidden from you a long time and I feel that it's something of which you now need to be made aware. It's very difficult for me to be coming out like this and I hope you will be gracious and understanding."

"Son, you can talk with me about anything. If it's something bothering you, I want to know about it so that I can help you find a solution."

"Thank you, Dad, that helps me to get this out a little easier. For as far back in my life as I can remember, I have struggled with my sexuality. I've kept it hidden from you and Mom as well as all my friends and classmates at school. Getting involved in sports and other apparent male activities was only a ploy to keep others from guessing my most closely guarded secret—my attraction to other males. For years I have lived with this loneliness and it wasn't until I first saw Finn that I was faced with the urgency of confronting my fears and seeking the comfort of another mate to help me rid myself of this dreaded vacuum. What I'm trying to say, Dad, is that I'm gay. For better or worse. I don't care what other people think anymore. It's better to live out who I am than to live a lie."

"Well, son, I won't pretend I'm not shocked at this news, but nevertheless I'm happy that you could get it off your chest. My initial response is to assure you that this doesn't change anything in my feelings toward you. I still love you just as much as I did before you told me this news. However, your confession has raised some questions that I wonder if you would clear up. For instance, why is it you needed Finn to come in here with you? Did he convince you to tell me about all this?"

"No, Dad, in fact the decision to break the news to you was a mutual agreement. Which brings me to the next part of my confession. Finn and I are lovers."

"How did that happen so quickly? You've only just met this week," Sam asked dumbfounded.

"Actually, I fell head over heals in love with him the first time I saw him three years ago in Dobersville when I was attending Collins business school."

"You mean you've known each other for three years? I'm incredulous! How can that be when I'm the one who found his résumé and hired him last week before you even met him."

"Finn, did you know Devin was my son when you sent me your application and you came in for your interview?" Sam looked intently at me for an answer.

"No I did not know it at the time, and when I met him here I was just as much shocked as you are now," I replied. But I could see my answer was not much help to poor Sam. I looked to Devin and said, "Perhaps you should explain what brought us together so we can dispel all this cryptic language and put it in a more believable context."

"Yes! Please do," Sam said.

"Perhaps when I tell you this, Dad," Devin began, "you'll begin, like us, to see the magic in the whole puzzle. It's been like a 'McGuffin' that began three years ago when I was attending Routers Business School in Dobersville. You recall at that time you offered to pay all my expenses, but I insisted you only take care of my tuition and that I wanted to cover the rest through seeking part time employment, which I did by getting a job as a delivery boy with the local Taco Bell. On one of my runs, in early September, I came up on a cabin in which Finn and his boyfriend Jake were staying. The front door was open while Jake went to get his checkbook, and I had a clear view into the kitchen where Finn was standing. The first time I saw him, I could not take my eyes off him. He looked up and caught me staring at him and being self conscious he moved out of my line of sight but not quick enough to prevent his unforgettable image from getting seared in my brain. From that day forward I prayed that one day him and me would be brought together. I told everybody at work that if any orders going to that cabin came in I wanted to be the one to deliver it."

"Months went by and Spring turned to Winter and the time was progressing fast toward my last day of working at Taco Bell. Then as luck had it, an order to that cabin came in and I grabbed it before the other driver could. All the way enroute I hoped I could see that boy again and then to my amazement he came out this time to receive the order. My heart was beating fast as I gave him the food and watched him put it on a table inside the door. Then as he was reaching into his pocket to get the gratuity, and my mind was racing like a marathon sprinter, in my desperation, I grabbed him and caught him off balance. Before he had the faculties to guess what was even happening, I drew him toward me and kissed him long and passionately on the lips. For a brief moment he did not pull away and we both felt something significant passing between us. Then suddenly he regained his presence of mind and struggled loose. He gave me a stern reprimand and warned he could have me fired. I just laughed and told him to keep the tip, the kiss was well worth it. Then I laughed and ran back to the truck shouting back it was my last day at work anyway."

"Years passed, and I wondered many times what had happened to him and Jake, but the memory of that kiss never allowed me to completely forget how it was holding him in my arms."

"Then you can imagine my shocked surprise when I walked into his office and saw him sitting there on Monday. Until that day I didn't even know his name. Consequently, when you gave me his résumé to read, I wasn't able to put the two together."

"Excuse me, Devin sweetheart, allow me to take it from here," I interrupted. "Sam, you remember at my interview I asked you what my duties would be here at Bernard-Severson and you instructed me that I would be paired with another exec to accompany me in going out to solicit new business? You informed at that time that I would be working with your son Devin. Since I never knew the name of that Taco Bell driver, I was totally unaware when he walked in the door of my office. All I knew was that he looked familiar, but I could not remember where we had met before. When I questioned him if we had met before, he gave me an evasive answer. I believe it was something like, 'Oh, I'm sure if I met someone as cute as you before, I wouldn't soon forget it.'

"He offered to take me to lunch for my first day as an opportunity for personal orientation. I questioned his academic background, and that's when he told me he attended classes at Routers Business School in Dobersville. When he mentioned Dobersville, it struck a chord in my mind because that was where Jake and I stayed at the cabin periodically. Then he told me he worked his way through school doing odd jobs as a delivery boy with fast food companies. That was when it all started coming back to me and he knew I had him. But when I considered how all these singular contingencies had come together by themselves, I was at a lost for any explanation. I had heard about serendipity before but never believed it could happen to me; yet I could not think of any other way to explain it. Even fate couldn't contain a strong enough argument to orchestrate this chain of events.

"Devin asked me what had happened with Jake and me, and why we weren't still together. I told him about the accident that killed him and his dad and how I was devastated and sent into a crippling depression for a little over a year.

"That was when Devin reached across the table to console me.

The touch of his hand somehow connected with that front porch kiss years ago and the loneliness I was chained to since Jake's death was replaced by the introduction of love once more. From that day on we both knew we were meant to be together and our relationship evolved quickly from friends to lovers.

Sam sat and listened with rapt fascination to our story. "You two are certainly meant to be together. No one could deny the force that forged you both from two to one. I love you both dearly, and I give you my blessing. There is however the working out of logistics because of the company's rules of relationships, but if you're willing to keep your association discrete, we can all live with it quietly, and no one needs to be any the wiser.

We left Sam's office feeling free from having to hide our secret attachment from him anymore. Everything was coming together nicely, and we felt that now nothing would be able to tear us apart.

CHAPTER 17

ALEX'S STORY

It was Friday afternoon, and Alex was getting ready to execute his plan to abduct Finn Bentley and add him to his list of gay murder victims. He knew he had to act fast. It was imperative that he move out of Philadelphia as quickly as possible. Moving shop westward into the interior of Pennsylvania would get him closer to his center of activity anyway. The little town of Moravia in central PA served well to be used for a hideout. Alex had inherited his grandmother's fortune three years ago after she had suspiciously fallen down the basement stairs and broken her neck. Now, with all of granny's lovely money, he had the means to build a custom home with all the amenities he needed for his sick pleasures. The main floor of his ranch style house was plain and simple, not betraying any illegalities. In fact, on the surface, even Alex's life resembled the picture perfect example of a man whose lifestyle was beyond reproach. He hid his compartmentalization well. But one had only to lift the braided carpet in the room he designated for his office and a trap door in the floor was discoverable that separated earth from purgatory. One had only to go down a short flight of stairs and a hidden basement with iron barred cages and instruments of torture and death awaited the next guest to visit Alex's inferno.

How, you might ask, could anyone be able to live with themselves, and at the same time, meet out these unspeakable acts of cruelty on another human being? Wouldn't their consciences alone condemn them? As truth has it, Alex had a history of sexual abuse perpetrated on him by his natural father which began when he reached 10 years of age. His feelings for his dad gradually deteriorated from love into hatred and then into deep resentment for the years of being exploited. His permanently scarred young mind already began formulating his adult mission of the abduction and murder of young homosexuals before they could develop into abusive dads like his father. When Alex's mother caught his dad in a homosexual act with another man in their bedroom, she packed up and left, leaving her husband with little Alex to raise by himself. That was when the abuses worsened over the next six years until Child Services got wind of it and removed Alex from the home and placed him under the care of his wealthy grandparents. Things went well with Alex from that point on until the death of his grandfather (his favorite of the two), and Grandma took over and ruled over him with an iron fist and rigid rules that Alex grew to hate. She held over him the threat of removing Alex from her will if he didn't comply with all her wishes and demands. When he found a copy of the will one day in Grandma's dresser, and read that he was first in line to inherit everything she had, he began planning poor Granny's accident. All it took was to maneuver her into place at the entrance of the open door to the basement, a little push, and the rest is history. The wooden stairwell was very unforgiving, and old Granny's neck snapped easily on her journey down to the basement floor.

But getting back to the present, all Alex's plans were contingent on his being successful in capturing and escaping with cute little Finn Bentley. He had a knife with an eight-inch blade concealed under his jacket if it became necessary to put down any resistance, also his taser in a neat little shoulder holster hung under his arm. He parked the van on the second floor of the garage and was able to catch the executive elevator to the seventeenth floor unnoticed. Getting Devin Elkins out of the way was his first priority. After that the rest would be a piece of cake.

CHAPTER 18

WHEN PLANS GO AWRY

Both Finn and Devin were looking forward to their first night alone together since Donna had left with the other ladies on tour and wouldn't be back until late Sunday evening. The time was creeping up on five o'clock, and Sam had left the building with his butler/chauffeur. The two lovers were the only ones left in the office and they were already eagerly anticipating the joy of embracing one another back at the apartment.

"Since we're leaving and won't be back until Monday," Finn suggested, "it might be best to take both our cars to my place tonight," Finn suggested. You never know what emergencies could transpire over the weekend."

"That's good thinking, Finn. It's always wise to have a plan B to fall back on should the unexpected happen and threaten to catch us off guard—especially with all the intrigue in our lives lately. Why don't you finish up here and I'll go down ahead of you and start both cars to warm them up."

"You're so thoughtful, hun. That's one of the first things I noticed about you and why I fell in love with you so quick," I complimented. "You go along and I'll be down shortly."

Devin got up and headed for the private elevator to the executive floor, which was out of the line of sight from Finn's office. He was unaware of Alex crouched behind the last row of desks near the door to the elevator. As he walked by, Alex jumped up and sunk his knife between Devin's shoulder blades. Devin felt a sting, followed by a sharp pain, as he fell suddenly forward to the floor in front of him. The last thing he remembered was the wetness filling the front of his shirt caused by the oozing of his own blood as he slowly lost consciousness. With Devin's intervention aborted, Alex stealthily made his way back to the outside of Finn's office. He overturned a chair that made a small ruckus but one just suspicious enough to cause Finn to get up from his desk and step out of his office door to investigate. That was all the opportunity that Alex needed as he touched his taser to Finn's bare neck causing his body to go into a state of neuromuscular incapacitation. He would have fallen to the floor had Alex not intervened and caught him on his way down. Then dragging him to his desk chair, he sat him down, secured him in it with duct tape, and then began wheeling it back to the private elevator door. Alex carefully maneuvered the desk chair facing away from the bleeding Devin on the office floor to keep Finn from getting too unmanageable when the effect of the taser finally began wearing off. On the fourth floor of the parking garage, he cut away the duct tape, opened the rear door of the van, pushed the still traumatized Finn onto the van floor, and hand-cuffed his wrists to custom metal rings fastened tight to the ve-hicles inside walls. Then he ran around the front of the van, jumped in the driver's seat, drove down the ramps of the garage, and out into the street heading towards the turnpike. Once he got on the highway, it was an hour and a half drive west to exit 24, Moravia, and his bunker in the secluded area of the woods.

Meanwhile Officers Waddell and Randal were getting anxious because neither Finn nor Devin had come down from the office yet.

"Maybe we should go up there an investigate to make sure everything is alright," Randall suggested.

At that they both boarded the elevator and pressed the button for the seventeenth floor. The ping sounded, and the door open on their destination. As soon as they stepped out the door they spied Devin lying unconscious on the floor in a pool of blood. Waddell ran over to him and checked his vitals to see if he was alive.

"He still has a pulse, but it's weak. Randall, call 911, and send for the paramedics. I'll go and check Mr. Bentley's office to see if he's alright."

"He's not here," Waddell yelled back to his partner. "I'll call Sandy and see what she wants us to do."

By now the paramedics had arrived and carefully put the un-conscious Devin on a gurney and were taking him to St. Mary's Hospital where he was immediately admitted to the emergency room.

As soon as Sandy was briefed on all the latest events, she called the FBI and filled them in on the facts. Local police and FBI officers don't usually have a good record of working together, but Sandy was not one to sacrifice the wellbeing of an abducted party just to satisfy her past prejudices. Besides, the Bureau had way more superior resources to draw from than the police.

Bill Hadley and Sandy had a relationship that went back a few years. In fact, before Bill left the police force, he had Sandy's job and she was his assistant. When he was offered his present job with the Bureau, he made sure that Sandy was promoted to his old position as head police detective. He and Sandy had been already linked up on the Alex Wilkes's files in connection with the three murders of young homosexuals in Maryland, Delaware, and Pennsylvania. Alex had lived in the same vicinities as the three other abductions and murders. That, along with the eye witness account of his recent failed victim who escaped out of his car after first singeing his left arm with the lit cigarette lighter, they had enough evidence against him to arrest him charge him on a capital offense.

Bill was able to produce a complete dossier on all Wilkes's activities.

"Here's his history from the time he turned sixteen and Child Services placed him in the custody of his grandparents where he remained until he turned eighteen. Anything before that is in sealed records since he was a minor at the time. We can track all purchases since then by his social security card and bank records. He inherited six million dollars left to him in the will of his grandmother. He built an expensive custom home near Moravia, PA. This could be, by the way, where he is taking Finn Bentley, since it is in a very secluded area of the woods. Here's a copy of the blueprints submitted by the contractor. It appears that he has a full basement. Very likely loaded with macabre instruments that he uses for his sadistic tortures. I hate to think what he has planned to do to young Finn if we don't stop him first. We still have enough time to send a SWAT team ahead in a helicopter and bag the bastard as soon as he gets there."

"Bill Hadley! You're my hero!" Sandy said, looking at him admiringly. "Now, let's go get him."

CHAPTER 19

THE TRIP TO MORAVIA.

The long hour and a half drive to Alex's bunker allowed Finn some time to think about an escape plan. By now the stunning from the taser had almost completely worn off.

A myriad of fearful thoughts ran through my head. "What if I'm not able to free myself from this sick individual? What has happened to Devin? Did Alex ambush and kill him on his way down to the cars? If I die, what will become of Mom? Who will take care of her in her old age? And what about poor Sam?" We hadn't had the chance to confide in him about all this. He wasn't even aware that all this was going down. How awful it would be if he lost Devin now? He's all he has left since his wife died and left him. I've never prayed to God before, but maybe it's time to think about it more seriously.

The transition from the smooth highway to the rough country road had now become noticeably evident.

"Wherever Alex is taking me, I'm afraid it will be where no one will be able find me. I mustn't let myself be discouraged. He may have the upper hand now, but I refuse to go down without a fight. The lives of too many others are at stake. I can't just think of myself. I can't just give in."

Suddenly, the pavement under the wheels got smooth again and I surmised we had pulled up onto a driveway. Alex shut the van off, and I could hear him open the cab door and get out. I heard the door shut again, and I noticed his footsteps coming around to open the rear doors to get me out. The horror in the realization that I was in the captivity of a mad man threatened to overwhelm my emotions, but then I pushed it aside as unproductive thinking. I must come up with a plan. If he doesn't taser me again, but just unshackles me first, I'm going to fight him with all the force I can muster.

Suddenly I heard the shouting of other voices. I could tell that there were more than one. At least three different ones were shouting warning commands.

"Alex Wilkes, FBI. You're under arrest. Keep your hands where we can see them. Get down on your knees with your hands behind your head."

While one agent was walking the handcuffed Alex to their car, another one had opened the back door of the van and was freeing me from the shackles on my hands and feet.

"You're free now, Finn," he spoke with soft manly comfort in his voice. Those were the sweetest words I had heard all day.

My eyes were blurry, and tears of joy ran down my cheeks. My ordeal was over, and yet I knew that it wouldn't be completely over until I knew what had happened to Devin. I prayed that he was safe.

I questioned the agent for any news about Devin. He said all he knew was that Mr. Elkins was taken to the hospital unconscious from a knife wound. My heart sank, and I begged whatever deity was in charge of the living to save him and not let him die.

CHAPTER 20

HELICOPTER RIDE TO ST. MARY'S

The copter pilot offered me a ride to St. Mary's hospital. We landed on the roof's helicopter pad and I got out and ran in the doors to the elevator. Sandy was waiting there to meet me with tears in her eyes. My heart sank again thinking those tears were because of bad news.

"I'm so glad we could rescue you from that monster," Sandy cried.

"Have you any news of Devin?" I asked impatiently.

"He was moved from ER to ICU an hour ago," Sandy said. "He hasn't regained consciousness yet and he's lost a lot of blood. They have been able to ascertain that the knife wound missed all his vital organs though. I'll be honest with you, Finn, it's still touch and go. All we can do is hope. Come on, I'll take you to him now."

Sandy's help and comforting manner was turning the two of us from merely a professional relationship into a real friendship that I knew would outlast this present ordeal. She grabbed my hand and squeezed it as a show of support on the elevator ride up to the third floor. She knew the room and she knew the way so she was able to guide me right to Devin's bedside.

When I saw Devin all hooked up to life support wires, I almost collapsed from the shock. His eyes were shut and he lied there in unconscious sleep. Guilt swept over me, and I vented it out on pour Sandy.

"I blame myself for this," I said to Sandy. "If it wasn't for me Devin would not have been there when Alex came to get me. He wouldn't be lying here in a hospital bed unconscious and hanging on dearly for his life."

"Don't do that to yourself," Sandy assured me. "No one can predict what a psychopath like Alex is going to do. There is no way a person can prepare for the unknown. These kinds of people are driven by their lower animalistic natures. Besides, he had concocted his plan to get you before you even went in for your interview with Sam Elkins."

"Oh yes! I am dreading it, but I need to call Sam so he can come over here.

He'll probably blame me for getting his son in this trouble," I said worried.

"He's already been here and left again," explained Sandy. "I've already sat with him and filled him in on the whole story. He knows all about Alex's reading the private files on you at night in the office and how he decided then and there to make you his next target. You don't have to worry about him blaming you either; he's taken more than enough responsibility for the whole mess. He blames himself for leaving your file out where Alex could get to it and start his little reign of terror. Before he left he said he owed you a great apology."

Before Sandy could finish, we heard the elevator ping, and a dejected looking Sam came walking toward us. When he saw me, he came right up to me, hugged me, and kissed me on the cheek.

"My dear Finn, you can't know how sorry I am for all that has happened to the both of you."

When I realized that he was not blaming me, and that I still held his respect, I hugged him back and told him, with tears of relief running down my cheeks, not to blame himself, and that Alex is the only one here who is to blame.

"We have all suffered equally and we will get through it together. If you will stay here awhile and keep watch, I have something I must do and I'll be back shortly."

CHAPTER 21

ADVERSITY GROWS THE MUSCLES OF FAITH

Sam watched curiously as I walked over to the nurses station and asked her something quietly. Then I got into the elevator going down to the first floor.

When the doors opened again, I stepped into to the corridor, turned to the left, and followed it to the end of the hall. There I found I was facing two beautifully carved wooden doors that led me into a quiet room with eight rows of benches on either side of a soft carpeted aisle. At the front of the room was a life-sized statue of Jesus with his arms raised and outstretched. I made my way to the front row of pews and took a seat. I've never considered myself to be religious; I've never even been in a church before. But I have studied enough about church history to know if I prayed for anything today, I wouldn't be praying to an idol, but instead the person who this statue represented.

I sat there quietly thinking about what I was going to say. Finally in a low voice I offered up my plea for Heaven's help.

"Dear God, I've heard others say you can do anything. Well today I am asking you for a miracle. As you know, a few years ago my first lover Jake was taken from me in a tragedy before I had the opportunity to ask you to save him." Tears started flowing down my cheeks, and my words were having to be forced out of a choked throat. "Now it's Devin who is in need of your healing, and I have been brought here on my knees before you tonight to beg you to spare his life. Many others have said you are a God of grace. Please forgive us sinners and help us to find a way to live a life more pleasing in your sight. You are my only hope now, and I trust your mercy will preserve us both." A strange calm had come over me, and I suddenly had the peace to believe that everything was going to be okay.

Just then my cell phone buzzed and my attention was drawn to a text sent from Sandy that read: "Finn, We don't know where you are right now, but you must come back up to Devin's room right away."

Calmly, I got up and walked out of that chapel, down the hall to the elevator, hit the up button, and waited for the ping. I got in and selected the third floor, and rode up, not knowing what to expect, but sensing that either way I would have the strength to accept it.

As I walked down the hall to Devin's room, there were nurses running in and out of the door excitedly. When I entered I saw Sam and Sandy standing next to Devin's bed with tears of joy running down their faces. Devin was sitting up in bed with a big smile when he saw me come in. At that point I didn't care who may have been watching, but I ran to his bedside and gave him a long thankful kiss on his lips.

The doctor came in and ordered the nurses to remove all the life support equipment. He shook his head in unbelief at Devin's rapid recovery.

"I've never seen this happen before," he said. "I've heard of miracles, but this is the first one I witnessed first hand."

Devin looked at me and winked with a twinkle in his eye.

"Hey, doc, do you think I could go home tonight?"

"No. I think you should at least spend the rest of the night here. Tomorrow is Saturday. I'll be back in the morning. We'll talk about it then."

"Can I at least have Finn stay with me overnight?"

"Yes! In fact I've already instructed the nurses to move you out of ICU to a private room on the fourth floor. I'll have them wheel in a second bed for your boyfriend."

After the doctor left, we all talked about how Alex had been arrested and put in jail without bail.

Sandy said, "This has been a Friday to go down in history as the year's fastest moving events. I'm so emotionally drained, I feel like I could sleep for a week."

Sam said, "I'm just thankful to God that things turned out the way they did. Sandy! Why don't you and I go home and leave these two lovers alone."

"Sounds good to me," Sandy agreed.

Later when we were moved to the private room with two beds in it, Devin and I cuddled up together in his bed and slept peacefully in each other's arms all night.

Sam had ordered breakfast for two to be delivered to our room so we didn't have to rely on eating hospital food. There was a note that came with it saying he wanted us to take off from work Monday so that we could have a day of rest and be back to work on Tuesday, my lucky day. After breakfast we sat and talked while we waited for the doctor to come in.

"Have you contacted your mother about all that has been going on?" Devin asked.

"No! I didn't want to spoil her trip with the ladies from the book club. Besides, she would have worried and swamped me with annoying calls for updates every hour. I'll fill her in when she gets back on Sunday evening. Is she going to get an earful?" I laughed. "We can at least have our night alone together that we've been waiting for. That is if the doctor says you can go home today."

"Oh, I'm getting out of here today, with or without his permission," Devin stated.

"Whoa! Tiger! You've been through a lot. It's best to let the doctor make the call," I cautioned.

"Really, Finn, I feel fine. I can be resting up at your place just as easily as I could be here. Well, that is for one exception." He winked.

His wink was so masculine, I wanted to throw myself into his arms and have him make love to me right then and there. But, just then the doctor came into the room. He looked at Devin, shook his head again in unbelief, and after a cursory examination pronounced him good enough to be released. We didn't wait for a second opinion. We started packing his things right away, and called for a wheelchair to take him to the front desk to be checked out. The nurse at the desk seemed regretful to see him leave.

"It isn't often we get such a handsome guest," she commented.

What did she think we were? Two brothers, cousins, friends? How could she have missed that we were a gay couple. I just rolled my eyes and started wheeling him to the elevator. Sandy had seen to it that my RAV4 was brought to the parking lot last night. Her friendship was becoming so warm. I was determined that her and I would be a lot closer friends in the days ahead.

After I had loaded my treasure into the passenger seat of the car, we drove straight to Bonnieville Arms.

CHAPTER 22

BACK AT THE SAFE HOUSE

Even though it had been only 24 hours since we left the apartment yesterday, the warm feeling of safety pervaded the place as soon as we walked through the front door. The whole harrowing ordeal was finally ended, and we had emerged the victors—still alive, still together, and with a stronger bond than ever before. It was hard to believe that all of it happened in a 24-hour time period. We had met with John Welch and landed his sporting goods account. After which Devin and I had outed to his dad about his being gay and our love relationship. Then there was Devin's stabbing attack that almost killed him. Followed by my tasing and abduction that ended up with the FBI capturing Alex and securing my release. Then worst of all was the long night vigil in the hospital, not knowing if Devin was going to live or die from being knifed and losing so much blood.

Thankfully, now we had arrived home at noon and I sat him down and began preparing a light lunch for the both of us. A grilled cheese sandwich and a green leaf salad was just the ticket. A small amount of red wine was great to top it off with. While we were sitting at the table eating lunch and enjoying each other's company, I noticed that poor Devin's eyelids were beginning to droop, and at one point he almost fell off the chair sideways.

"Sweetheart!" I called to him from across the table. "Why don't we go and lie down on my bed and nap for a while. Your body is probably crying out for rest after last night's fray."

We knew it wasn't what we both wanted to do, but it was what should do. As soon as he hit the mattress he was fast asleep. While he slept I left him undisturbed for the next six hours during which time I went to my computer and began writing my memoirs about the many events that have taken place since my starting to work at Bernard-Severson. As I wrote, I kept thinking that my readers would find it hard to believe a whole week of surprises could be condensed into such a short period of time. At five o'clock I shut off the computer and went to work on getting dinner ready for us.

At 5:45 Devin came out the bedroom, walked straight over to me, embraced me, and gave me a long and passionate kiss. All I could think about was how wonderful to know he was mine for the rest of my life and I'd never be lonely again.

Finally, when dinner was over, we retired to my bedroom to continue what we had left unfinished yesterday. The love we now originally felt for each other had deepened dramatically since the harrowing events we had recently been taken through. At last we melted in each other's arms and the afterglow from the kiss that we shared on the front porch of the cabin years ago had now taken on its fullest expression in our deep rooted love for one another.

Epilogue

Sunday morning we woke up cuddling together. Unexpectedly, I began recalling the petition I had made in the chapel Friday night when I asked God to forgive us and help us to find the way to live our lives more pleasing in his sight. It entered my mind to suggest to Devin that, after all we had been through, we should perhaps find a church to attend and start adding a little religion to our lives. But then I opted to save it for a more opportune time. Instead we should be getting ready for Mom's return home from her tour. We decided to play it cool, not knowing the exact time she'd be coming through the door. As it turned out, she arrived earlier than expected.

The sound of her key in the door lock alerted us she was home. A moment later, and she was standing in the apartment bubbling over with the news of her trip. Devin offered to help her carry in her baggage, but she explained that Roger was downstairs retrieving all the luggage from the bus and would be up shortly to deliver.

"Well hello, you two," she said with exuberance. "It was so much fun on this trip I can't wait tell you all about it. I'm sure you must have had a long and boring weekend without me around," she said coyly. Devin and I exchanged amused glances and let her have her fun.

"Yes, Mom! We had very dull time here while you were gone," I said playfully, winking at Devin. "But you go first and tell us about your exciting experiences in New York City and then we want you to get comfortably seated when we get our turn to tell you all about our *boring* weekend."

THE END

www.ingramcontent.com/pod-product-compliance
Lightning Source LLC
Chambersburg PA
CBHW050752160726
48004CB00002B/529